HERE THERE BE MONSTERS

THE SYMBICATE 3

THE BEAST IN THE VOID

SEAN M. T. SHANAHAN

CHAPTER 1

The Beast

Out of the void, the Beast emerged.

It swam deep, *deep* within the abyss of space, a leviathan shrouded in the rippling wisps of the nebula it fed on. Celestial debris churned out of its path like water would churn from the bulk of an unfathomable beast in the dark sea.

As it emerged from the stellar depths, it was followed. Objects trailed from it in an orbiting path, tearing after it through the streaks of debris puffing in its wake. The detritus of conflict scattered into the trailing abyss as battles still raged.

The thing turned void-wards, to the great nothing that rested beyond the shore of the stars—food was so scarce this far from the centre. Its vast maw crushed a planetoid that strayed into its path. It spat the granules of the would-be world from tectonic teeth and propelled itself towards a peculiar little sun well that clung to the edge of the galaxy.

The sun well had two fully formed worlds that teemed with life … but there was nothing for it to feed on there, nothing as bountiful as nebula. This well was older and more stable than the feeding grounds the Beast would trawl, the sun expelled nothing of substance, nothing new … but the compulsion to swim towards it was immense.

Or was it subtle?

It mattered not to the Beast; it was a compulsion all the same.

But this one was other, it was dark, it needled into its mind, wormed into its joints.

It was not itself.

It resisted.

But it was not some compulsion to be tossed aside. This compulsion was from The Rel, which had infected its mind. The Rel wanted it to barrel towards these worlds that were the last vestige of the Symdian's pets, defended by motley bands of defiant little things.

The Rel was coming for them, and it was coming for their doom.

CHAPTER 2

Tara Star

It was a strange sensation, turning into light.

Tara gaped in wonder and splayed her fingers as they wavered into luminescence. The *Motebeam* shuddered, and Tara and Snipes both flinched as the edges of the bridge began to pulse and fluctuate.

Mallel watched and smirked briefly, but turned back to his crew. "Status, Miss Votly?" His voice was deep and commanding; it rattled with the shimmering air.

"Wave-Form drive is ready to fire, sir. Just say the word." Votly looked up from her console. A wisp of seaweed-green hair caressed her peach brow with the motion. "Um, are they all right?"

Mallel turned back to Tara and Snipes.

As the Wave-Form engine did its borderline magical work, the two newcomers had very different reactions. Fractal waves of light warbled along the floors, up the walls, and along the ceiling as polyps of incandescent stuff precipitated from their skin.

Snipes doubled over while clutching at his belly and stumbling over the seemingly translucent floor. But Tara was giggling. She pirouetted with splayed arms; her leather coat twirled, and wisps of her light brown hair danced in the cascading fractal light.

"I must say," Mallel said, "you are handling this a lot better than even trained Wave-Form sailors on their first transmutation."

Tara stopped mid-spin and homed in on the captain. The polyps of light made his silver hair shine, and the beams reflected off his pitch-black skin as if it was metal.

"I've had a lifetime of forced training." Tara shrugged in response. "You're either graceful or you die."

Mallel nodded almost imperceptibly.

Almost.

Tara narrowed her eyes at him; they still had not the measure of each other—other than as enemies quickly turned allies due to a common foe. The silence between them passed as Snipes suffered his episode of unease at the changing from mass into light under the power of the Light Wizards.

Finally, one of the technicians—Bromean, a lean, bronze-skinned figure—broke the contest between Tara and Mallel by uttering what some of the crew was thinking. "Trained to be a killer, that's who you've brought onto our ship."

Tara's gaze faltered, an event that stunned Mallel more than the insubordination from his crew. The fleeting moment of terror that danced through her eyes infuriated him more than anything.

Mallel rounded on Bromean before Tara could bite back with what would undoubtedly be a scathing and just comment. "Did we not sack an entire city while she scrambled for cover within it? Are we not the killers you claim her to be? Much worse, I say. We almost committed genocide."

"We had a mission!" Bromean retorted. "You would do it all over again under similar circumstances!"

Votly and the other technicians on the bridge tried to make themselves smaller, shrinking over their consoles.

"We had a duty," Mallel corrected, "a responsibility to do the right thing, for the right reasons; and when it mattered, we faltered. Tara and her companions' retribution was warranted."

"And who ordered the strafing of that infested sewer, Captain?" Bromean spat the last word. "Who let onto this ship an assassin who is woven with not one, but two creatures that the Rel can infect?"

Mallel didn't answer—not with his voice at least—instead he stalked over to Bromean. The polyps of fractal light cascaded over his silver hair and accented his dark brow in such a foreboding manner that Bromean found the mutiny shrivelling up within him.

"Will that be all?" Mallel said, finally ... mercifully.

Bromean's lip quivered, but he nodded.

"Then engage the Wave-Form, and send us to our destination. Now."

Bromean turned in his swivelling chair and keyed the sequence. The *Motebeam* hummed and pulsed with increasing pitch and frequency before finally shooting from the world in the form of the technicoloured comet that first brought them to this planet's atmospheric shores.

Mallel nodded to himself, almost imperceptibly again. But his inner confidence churned as he turned back to his two new passengers. Tara was staring at him again, this time with venom—such a sudden and frightening change from her air of whimsicalness beforehand. He could not help but note the tinge of red on her cheeks, flushed with anger. It was strange to him that the people from her world had red blood instead of blue.

She was clutching Snipes to help him stand. "We will be at our quarters, Captain ... lest you or your crew order more hostilities against us," she said coolly.

Mallel opened his mouth to speak, but Tara was already half dragging Snipes out the sliding doors of the bridge and down the chrome hallways to the quarters they had been provided.

Mallel sighed.

"She's a good match for you, that one," Votly sighed with him.

"Excuse me?" Mallel's cheeks flushed with blue blood; thankfully the strobing lights hid it from view.

Votly squeaked involuntarily as Mallel focused his practiced, authoritative gaze on her.

"What I mean to say is ..." she floundered, "is that I don't know none other than the High Prismatist who could withstand your glare. If you don't mind me saying ... sir."

Mallel's glare fractured for a second as he smirked. "Indeed. We are all saddened for his passing. Not only was he a hero but a mentor and leader. Much of his craft died with him. I know you feel his loss dearly, Votly. He would have been a great help in mitigating the issues we face here on this ship today." He glanced at Bromean, who was doing a terrible job of pretending not to listen to the conversation. "As it is, I am all that remains to lead us into the void. And by that power, if any harm comes to our new comrades, I shall have more than words with the perpetrators."

Bromean stiffened, but again, said nothing in challenge.

It was a good enough response, Mallel thought, considering all that they had been through ... for now.

"Captain," the helmsmen called from the wheel. "Our course is solid. We're making way to the outer sun well and should intercept the anomaly we detected within a week Wave-Form time."

Mallel nodded and turned to Votly. "Is the assessment accurate?"

"Yes, sir." Votly typed at her console. "Whatever the anomaly is, though, it's hard to get a read on. We best prepare for anything."

"I have faith in our crew," Mallel said. "I just hope they maintain their faith in each other."

* * *

Snipes was not a bulky man; in fact, he was quite slender—if a bit tall—and full of lean, wiry muscle. But even with her hardened resolve, Tara found it hard to carry him with his arm around her lithe shoulders.

The only other person from my world, and he's too seasick ... void sick, to be of any use to me in a pinch.

He mumbled something incoherent and tightened his grip on her as they stumbled down the chrome hallways.

9

"If you vomit on my jacket, I'll boot you over the edge of this infernal vessel," Tara muttered.

Snipes muttered something back.

The hall was thankfully more opaque than the bridge; perhaps they were more insulated in these sections. Here it wasn't necessary to know you were flying across the stars at insane speeds.

Tara swiped open the door to their chambers, a quaint cabin with a bunk bed and the amenities of plumbing and storage ... with the added benefit of the extra technology the Light Wizards possessed.

"I usually like the top bunk," Snipes said as she gently rolled him onto the bottom one. "Shooting from high places and all that."

"And I like to backflip out of bed." Tara smiled. "And you ain't sleeping on top of me until you get your sea legs, Snipes ... or should I call you David?"

"Snipes is fine," he said, breathing with puffed cheeks as his pale skin turned a shade of green.

"Snipes is probably better." Tara chuckled.

"I agree."

"Snipes ... I know you and Thomas had your hang-ups ... but we are going to need to trust each other, watch each other's backs if other members of the crew still see us as foe."

"Again, I agree." Snipes made the awful guttural noise of someone about to spew out their innards, but nothing came.

"So, why can't you handle this? I recall you giving Thomas a lot of crap when he was nervous to be at heights."

"It's the shimmering, the warbling. I don't mind heights; need them to do my thing. But solid ground, I need solid ground. It's a stupid thing based off a bad mistake I made once." His ill voice hardened for a moment back to his more natural, steadfast Soth accent. "I just need solid ground beneath my feet or I start to choke up."

Tara reached out to caress his red hair, hesitated, and then thought there was no harm in it. "Hush now then, Snipes. This journey won't last too long, and when we arrive wherever it is we're going, there'll be some place you can set up your roost."

Snipes mumbled incoherently again.

"You set out across the universe with only a stranger to right some wrong, I suppose. Let that be your solid ground. Even if the world crumbles around you, you will be unshakable."

Snipes stilled, and nodded before the mumbling returned.

Tara hushed him. "I'll look out for you, and you'll look out for me ... until we can get a measure of our new company." Her thoughts flashed back to the stare-down with Mallel. The way he stood up for her, the way he challenged her gaze. The tingling of her Luck Symbioid crept down her spine; it was trying to tell her something, something about Mallel ... *But he ordered the attack on Crankod.* She stood from her perch on the edge of Snipes's bunk and clambered into her own, lying over the tightly fitted sheets.

"I don't trust you," she said quietly, and the tingling flared again. "No, when you give me good luck, it gives bad luck to others... I don't trust you, Luck Symbioid. I held myself responsible for Regen's death, but it was *you*."

The tingling seemed to burn at her spine, but eventually it acquiesced, and Tara finally slept. Her dreams were plagued with burning cities, a floating ship—the one she now slept on—wreaking havoc, and Rella's insidious tendrils seeping barbs into her flesh.

* * *

To say that the two new members of the crew did not sleep well would be an understatement. Snipes and Tara had their own fever dreams while tossing and turning, but managed to last through the night without screaming or vomiting.

She considered that a good start to their voyage.

The next morning, they found themselves in the *Motebeam's* gymnasium. It was a large, low-ceilinged area where the chrome floors were replaced with cool cobalt plating. The deep blue flooring added a strange sense of darkness compared with the rest of the ship, but maybe those were just the dimmed lights. It was still early, and sleep encrusted their eyes. Tara battled the early signs of a headache, and Snipes continued to grumble as he checked over the different components of his modified blunderbuss.

The gymnasium was a large, square space set behind the cargo hold and above the thrumming engines. The cobalt floors and walls still vibrated and shimmered slightly from the effects of the Wave-Form process, but Snipes was in his element with his gun in hand. It took the edge off.

There was another crew member in the gymnasium. A prism marine, marked differently from the other Light Wizards on the ship with his stiff blue-grey coat. The marines seemed to be friendlier than the other caste of warriors on the *Motebeam*.

"That sure is a strange rifle you've got there." The marine grinned. He had pitch-dark skin—the same as Mallel—with

12

short-cropped green hair hugging his scalp. "My name is Balt, by the way. We didn't get much of a chance to introduce ourselves in the battle over that shattered city."

"Snipes," Snipes said.

"Tara," Tara replied.

"You two are great conversationalists." Balt chuckled as he sighted down the little shooting range, toggling the scope on his prism rifle.

"It's just been an adjustment period." Snipes donned his shooting goggles, slammed a shot cartridge into the bottom of his modified blunderbuss, and sighted down the short and bare shooting range on one end of the room. "Are there targets?"

"Sure there are." Balt lowered his weapon and hit a button on a control panel by the range. "It'll project a holographic target which will rush you, so you better be ready. You can't fire live rounds inside the ship ..." he gave Tara a pointed look, "unless we're boarded of course." He beamed another bright smile.

Tara couldn't help but smile innocently. "I was ..."

"Your hand was forced." Balt shrugged. "I'm just glad I didn't get to tango with you before we made nice."

Snipes quietly removed the cartridge from his weapon as they spoke. "Can the shooting range tell if I want to change the shot I'm using?" he asked.

"I really don't know," Balt said. "It can tell when you fire, I guess, but it really is suited to our weapons and not yours. What kind of shots do you have?"

"I have conical shots for longer distance targets, regular shots for everyday use, and flechette rounds for the odd time when people get too close."

"Wow," Balt whistled, "you don't need that with this pretty thing." He tapped the prism rifle and grinned. "You ready?"

Snipes nodded.

Balt hit another button, and the shooting range darkened. A shape made of light materialised and sprinted towards them. Snipes raised his blunderbuss and pulled the trigger; the shape disintegrated in response to his motion. More shapes emerged, and Snipes squeezed the trigger in quick succession, each quiet click disintegrating another ghostly phantom.

"There's no recoil," he muttered.

"Our prism rifles don't have recoil. They just thrum a bit," Balt said between shots of his own. "Want me to get you one instead of that clumsy slug thrower?"

"No thanks!" Snipes half laughed, half shouted. "The only weapon I use is mine."

The gymnasium doors slid open, and another marine marched in, a woman with pinkish-hued skin and copper-coloured hair. Snipes paused from firing to watch her approach—long enough that one of the holographic targets rushed him, and the simulation terminated with a buzzer tone.

"Flayr distracted you, eh?" Balt nudged him.

"Cool your boiler." Snipes chuckled.

Tara rolled her eyes and moved away from the range as the newcomer—Flayr—came over and introduced herself to Snipes before she took up position beside him and started shooting. Tara instead made for the sparring mats, finding the panel that sprouted from the floor on one side supported by a chrome rod. She gave the panel an experimental wave, and a display danced across the monitor. She still struggled not to think of the monitors as magic windows, or lenses. It was also important that she stop thinking of the people on this ship as Wizards: the people from their world had a name—the Prismath—and it was their technology that made them seem so magical.

The displays dancing across the monitor indicated different simulations with Prismath symbols of varying colours. Tara supposed the colours indicated the skill required to participate in them.

She looked up as the sliding doors into the gymnasium opened and a group of Prismath riflemen walked in. The riflemen were soldiers like the marines but dressed in drab brown. There were more of them than the marines, and based off her encounters with them so far, they were less disciplined.

They regarded her warily as she turned her attention back to the simulation panel—ignoring them.

She swiped through the different arrangements until she found the one marked with amber characters—her Luck Symbioid tingled, a warning she ignored—and hit it.

The matting area dimmed marginally, and little projectors on the ceilings started to shine, emitting the Wave-Form shapes she would be battling.

Tara breathed deep, cracked her neck, and stepped into the centre of the mat.

The first image rushed her without warning, making to slam its shoulder into her throat. Tara brought up her arms to grapple the thing around her—these things had mass, light turned into matter through the all but magical power of Wave-Form technology—but she was floored by the sheer momentum it slammed her with.

With a breathless grunt she was slammed onto her back, and through instinct alone she rolled out of the way of the stamping foot of the hologram to rush her next. She kipped up onto her feet, pushing off the ground with her shoulders as she whipped her feet down to the ground, and decided that warming up with hand-to-hand combat would not do for today.

She drew two throwing knives from the webbing in her coat and spun with them in an underhanded grip, jabbing and slicing at the would-be stomper.

Flecks of light splintered from the image as she struck at it. They flaked off like sparkling dust, and the hologram fell back, imitating the need to defend itself. The one that shoulder-charged her swooped around to flank her. She spun, savaging it with a hook kick that shattered its face and sent a dull ache shooting up her leg and through her hip.

The image fell, shattering to bits before two more simulated enemies were generated to replace it.

Tara's eyes widened. *Probably should have asked what the markings meant before I started this,* she realised. She slashed at the throat of the one she had harassed into a retreat, and it, too, shattered, to also be replaced by another two images.

They swarmed her at once, and Tara reached for a smoke bomb—realising she had not carried them into the gymnasium. She ducked under one hooking blow to be kicked off her feet by the next, and the four images descended on her, mobbing her like a pack of brawling drunks. Each blow was like a hammer, bruising organs, rattling bone, and the tingling intensified.

"No," she grunted, but she had no control over the symbioid's need to help her.

Someone shouted something, and the simulation ended with a droning hum, the holograms fading away. Tara squinted through pain-bleared eyes to find Votly had rushed into the gymnasium and slammed her hands on the emergency stop button.

"Why did you do that?" Tara croaked, pushing up from the ground, ignoring the protests of her battered body through the sheer experience of ignoring them during her youth.

"I got the warning someone activated the gauntlet match without a spotter!" Her usually airy voice was even more breathless from her sprinting.

"What?"

"The simulation you started isn't winnable; it's meant to test our soldiers before combat to see how long they can last in a hopeless situation. Someone has to terminate the match before the soldiers die." Votly rushed into the mat, checking Tara for wounds even as she battered her off.

"I was fine!"

A derisive snort sounded from one of the other training mats. "Sure."

Tara looked over to find the group of riflemen watching idly. They had positioned themselves to be between Tara and the firing range, Tara realised. Snipes would have had no idea what danger she was in.

"Why didn't you step in?" Votly cried in a shrill tone.

"Hey, Techie, you don't get to talk to riflemen like that." The lead rifleman puffed his chest and stalked over to Votly, pushing into her with his gait. He had bronze skin, matted green hair, and a smug, pointed expression.

Oh great, Tara lamented as she stood up. *A hot-headed boiler brain.*

"She could have died!" Votly slapped the rifleman across the face.

The riflemen quieted as the slap echoed across the gym.

The rifleman she had slapped touched his cheek, fury dancing across his features. "You dare strike me, you little ..."

Tara rolled her eyes and pushed herself between Votly and the rifleman, spitting blood onto the mat. "You wanna cool your boiler there, pal?"

He sneered down at her, a lock of green hair falling across his golden brow. "Cool my boiler? You cracked primitive."

"Primitive?" Tara echoed. "Maybe we would be a bit primitive when people from your world blew up our moon. What's your problem?"

"You're our problem," one of the other riflemen piped up. "You don't belong here."

"Then take that up with your fearless leader," Tara shot back. "I'm here to kill the Rel, but I'll beat you all into a pulp while I'm at it if I have to."

"You don't fight fair," the lead rifleman grunted. "You wouldn't beat us into a pulp; you'd put us on the ground and burn us to death."

Tara suppressed a gasp, and images of the Prismath rifleman from the battle at the Baul Islands flashed through her mind. It wasn't just the image; it was the smell of burning flesh, the sound of his last pained breaths as he tried to writhe away from her. She suppressed a sob, suppressed the compulsion to apologise for what she did, but then similar sensations flooded through her, detailing the devastation of Crankod.

Exploding buildings, thousands of screaming people, men, women ... children. And the flood that followed the artillery fires as the weir broke and the city crumbled into the River Barcos.

Tara's voice came out a harsh, even whisper. "Was that before or after he burned a city of children alive?"

The rifleman didn't answer. He simply grimaced, then threw a punch.

Tara saw it coming and ducked under it, meaning to grapple him to the ground with his own momentum like she had tried with the Wave-Form hologram. This time it worked. After she slammed him on the ground, she twisted his arm for good measure until it popped out of his shoulder with an audible click and pained cry.

The other riflemen rushed in, and the brawl spilled back onto the mat as Votly shouted uselessly at them to stop from the sidelines.

At some point, Snipes, Balt, and Flayr rushed in, pulling the riflemen away from Tara as she laid about them with a barely suppressed rage. In the end, they had to pull *her* off them instead.

Within her rage-and trauma-fuelled barrage, Tara was vaguely aware of a tall, imposing shape stalking into the room with a bark, and then of the Wizards who weren't savaged standing to attention.

It was Mallel.

"What in Shards is going on here?" He didn't shout, but his voice was deep and booming—it made his crew flinch.

She spat the extra blood out of her mouth, the crimson droplets spattering over the mats. "What?"

But Mallel was not looking at her; he was stalking up and down the line of antagonistic riflemen who had attacked her.

"We were just training, Captain," the instigator said.

Mallel stopped pacing and homed in on the belligerent. Tara was impressed that the rifleman managed not to shrink back under Mallel's gaze. "Training for what, Corporal Keihn?" Mallel asked. "Getting your asses handed to you by a single combatant?"

"She had hers coming," another spoke up, but *did* shrivel under Mallel's pointed glare.

"I thought we addressed this when the Stemcogs came aboard?" Mallel sighed.

"How can you expect us to let what she did go?" Keihn said.

"The same way she let go of what we did to the city she was in. Private Sreckle fell under her wrath, yes, as did others, but it was just. We almost all fell under her assault. You should be glad she showed mercy."

Tara stiffened at the name. *So now I have a name for the nightmares, Sreckle,* the rifleman she burned to death.

"Our wrath was just too!" Keihn protested.

"Just?" Mallel questioned. "Our intention was certainly just, but we missed the mark. So when does it end, Corporal Keihn?" Mallel leaned in over him. "When does it end?"

Keihn had no reply.

Tara was acutely aware that a whole manner of other marines had surged into the gymnasium. They were in their full battle dress with their navy-grey coats and angular helmets. The marines, Tara knew, were the more professional of the bunch, but there were fewer of them on board. She wondered how the Prismath kept control of the riflemen if they were so undisciplined.

Then she wondered when the marines would join the riflemen and attack her, but despite their guarded looks, they were more preoccupied with watching the riflemen.

"Seeing as you have nothing to say on the matter," Mallel said—Tara had forgotten they were still speaking—"you all have extra maintenance duties." He straightened and turned back to Keihn before he could speak out. "Dismissed, Corporal."

Grumbling, the riflemen marched out of the gymnasium, barging past the marines, who regarded them intently. Before the doors closed shut, Keihn shot a venomous look at Votly.

Mallel turned back to Tara, as Votly's concerned face popped over his shoulder. "Are you all right?"

"I didn't need your help," Tara said, wiping blue and red blood from her knuckles.

Mallel's demeanour softened with a smile—before his eyes flickered to the marines watching on—and it hardened again. "No, but my riflemen sure did need help." The marines chuckled.

Tara gave him a pointed look and then marched over to the sparring panel. "Well, is one of you going to show me how to set this to *not murder me* settings so I can let off some steam and not run up the walls in this accursed chrome tube you call a ship!"

"Oh, are you experiencing cabin fever?" Votly's squeaking voice sounded as she sidled up to the panel and started swiping through the combat readouts. "Once we leave Wave-Form I can take you out for a void swim if you like?"

"A what?" Snipes leaned in.

"A void swim. We put you in a suit, and you can drift out in the vacuum outside the *Dustmote*."

"No thank you!" Snipes raised his hands and stepped back to the shooting range. "This ship is upsetting my stomach enough as it is. I don't need that kind of cogrusted agitation!"

Votly nodded and turned back to Tara, who was biting her lip. "You won't leave me to drift out there?" Tara said.

Mallel scoffed and turned from the room. His marines parted and let him through with salutes.

Votly eyed Mallel, making sure he left before she answered, and even then she leaned in conspiratorially. "I don't think Mallel would let me live if I lost you ..."

"Why? Does he want the honour of killing me himself?" Tara asked.

Votly blanched. "No, not at all. He takes your protection very seriously."

"Well, I need more information than that." Tara marched past Votly, through the marines, who scrambled to get out of her way, and out of the gymnasium. She stormed down the chrome hallways after Mallel while Votly scurried after her in her wake. "Hey!"

Mallel halted and turned, his eyes flashing wide for only an instant as Tara stormed up to him. "Yes, Miss Star?"

"What the hell is wrong with your crew? I know we were enemies for a hot second back on my world. But I'm trying *really* hard to let go of what you did to an entire gear-jammed city, and your people can't let go of my retaliation?"

Mallel inhaled and sighed deeply. He glanced at Votly, who nodded and scurried away. "Miss Star ... Tara."

"Yes?"

The silence passed between them, neither of them quite meeting the other's eye.

"The riflemen ... they did not choose to be here. They were encouraged by the government and people of Prisma. The prism marines all followed me willingly; they swore allegiances to wage a war on the Rel into the furthest reaches of the void if they had to. They were in the final battle against the Rel in our capital." He scrunched his eyes shut, his fists trembling.

Tara reached out to touch his arm but pulled back before he opened his eyes again.

"We had too few warriors for such a campaign. The riflemen were selected to bolster our ranks. The only reason they didn't desert us was because Scrond was joining them on the mission."

Tara took a moment to process that. "... Oh."

Scrond died in battle with Rella back in Copper Cobble on her world.

"Oh indeed," Mallel sighed. "It would not be an exaggeration to say he was the most respected man on our world ... and he died fighting your Rel in that overwhelmed city. He died doing what he set out to do ... but now the riflemen do not have their hero to keep them in check. All they have is me, the man who leads the expedition that they were forced onto, forced to leave their families behind for. Don't get me wrong, Tara, they know what is at stake, but that doesn't mean they like me, and it certainly doesn't mean they'll put up with you. The *Motebeam's* morale hangs by a thread. The rest of the crew try and stay out of the feud, but a few side with the riflemen in this."

"So ..." Tara crossed her arms. "I'm supposed to weather their ire?"

"It would help me greatly," Mallel said, "but I know that isn't who you are. I wouldn't have ..." He trailed off, stiffening again.

"You wouldn't have what?" Tara asked, the luck tingling spiking so much, it caused her voice to come out in an agitated gasp.

"Nothing ... excuse me, I have matters to attend to." Mallel turned from Tara, rounding the corner in the chrome hallway on his way to the bridge.

"Un-jam your gears!" Tara slapped her head. "I don't need you flaring every moment of my life!" The tingling flared and faded again. "No," Tara said, "I will not stop resisting you. You know why." But she could not stop thinking on what Mallel was about to say, could not stop thinking if he might have said it if she hadn't gasped like that. She gritted her teeth and turned back to the gymnasium.

* * *

Captain Mallel

Mallel stalked down the hallway, his calm demeanour belaying a hot rage that clung to his lungs and burned with every breath. Bromean was supposed to be monitoring the Stemcogs because he expected issues like this. If Votly hadn't looked over his panel, Tara could have been ...

His breath caught at the thought.

Silly really, she is capable ... His thoughts started to drift, but were cut short as he entered the bridge and sighted Bromean.

"Technician," Mallel barked. Bromean tried to glance away. "Do not ignore me, Void Sailor."

Bromean swivelled his chair around and stood to face Mallel, beads of sweat clinging to his skin. *Ah,* Mallel thought. *So he is nefarious and not incompetent.* "Do you have anything to say for yourself?"

"The men needed revenge," Bromean whispered.

The words were so quiet and so honest that Mallel stopped mid-stride, shocked, awed, furious. "She is a member of this crew now."

"Is she replacing the ones she killed?" Bromean clutched a data pad to his chest.

"How many times do we have to go over this?" Mallel all but shouted. "I feel like my marines are the only ones onboard with this."

"That's just it, *your* marines. They were handpicked by you, trained under you. The riflemen were lopped in with the rest of us to make up the numbers, to fire on that city under your orders and suffer the backlash ... they feel *betrayed.*"

"They were not conscripted," Mallel returned.

"But they would have lived in shame if they refused. How many broken lenses would have been left on their doorsteps by our women?" Bromean blustered.

"Bromean!" Mallel snapped. "Our world was *ravaged* by the Rel. I jammed my cutlass to the hilt into my own father's writhing body. I stood with Scrond as his fellow Prismatists were stripped of their flesh and dissolved in agony before our very eyes! And we knew the Rel was not defeated. The people of Prisma *knew* it had to be vanquished for good. I may not have approved of the way the young warriors were treated to go on this time-bending mission, but the people knew ... the people *know* that if we did not leave with full strength, we could not hope to defeat the Rel scions around the sun well. We lost good men and women in our folly at Stemcog; we can't lose the two who chose to come with us."

"Can't lose them as fighters, or you can't lose that pretty young one?" Bromean said.

"Get off my bridge!" Mallel snapped, his voice booming.

Bromean sighed and glanced down at the tablet in his hands; the strobing data on it reflected off his eyes, dissipating into the strobing walls and floor of the bridge. "Aye, Cap'n." He tapped something on the data pad and marched out.

Mallel took a deep breath and realised the other bridge crew were staring. "Well?"

They quickly turned back to their tasks.

CHAPTER 3

Votly

Votly clutched her holo-pad to her chest as she marched into the mess hall. The chattering din echoed to silence as the chrome doors slid open, and all that could be heard was the click clack of her boots across the hard flooring.

The eyes all followed her, from her fellow crew mates, the riflemen, marines, and from Tara and Snipes, who were sitting mostly to themselves on the far side of the hall. They were alone except for Flayr, who was cuddling up to Snipes, and for Balt, who was shovelling gruel into his mouth. He sat across from Tara, who silently sharpened one of her knives.

Votly moved to the head of the hall where a large screen was being lowered, and she cleared her throat.

"H-hello ..."

"We can't hear you!" one of the riflemen jeered, and laughter rippled throughout the hall.

"Maybe if you lot shut up!" A marine stood and shook her fist at them.

"Why don't you come and make me, Curla!" the rifleman retorted.

All of a sudden the echoed chatter of the mess hall came back in force as the marines and riflemen were on their feet and jeering, practically at each other's throats. Votly watched the chaos spread as her hands shook, holding the holo-pad tightly to her chest in order to hide her trembling.

"Um," she said, her voice lost in the raucous arguments that were erupting all along the hall. "Excuse me!" she stammered.

"Silence!" Mallel stormed into the mess hall, and again, the din died within an instant. "I believe Miss Votly was going to lead the meeting ..."

Mallel glanced at Votly, and then back to the gathered crew, his eyes lingering for just a moment on Tara—Votly noticed—before he strode to the empty chair at the officer's table and took a seat.

"Well," Votly cleared her throat again, "thank you for assembling. As you know, we are travelling towards the edge of the sun well to investigate an anomaly I detected of titanic proportions. We aren't sure how the Rel infected our moons to turn the guardians against us, but this could be a new wave. There is a benefit to our new course, though." Her voice squeaked, and she cleared her throat again as some of the riflemen sniggered. "We're travelling past our home world, and we've intercepted a number of transmissions."

Votly lowered her holo-pad and typed a few commands. The giant screen that had been lowered across the wall of the mess hall winked to life, and on it a learned old man with pinkish skin and greying green hair smiled at them.

"This is President Cortel. He would have taken over leadership of Prisma some five years after we left the planet. While travelling in Wave-Form, time moves much faster for the people we left behind, and our fellow Prismath have been broadcasting messages to our ship in the hopes that one day we may intercept them and have a record of our home ..."

The mess hall was so silent, you could have heard a pin drop.

"Yes," Votly continued, "there are personal messages from our families ... before they ... well, before they aged, and those have been sent to your respective holo-pads in your cabins. But there are a number of well wishes and updates from the entire planet as the decades have drawn on ... Ahem, so without further ado ... President Cortel!"

Votly played the message, and the image on the screen started talking, conveying words of gratitude and solemnity for the sacrifice the crew members of the *Motebeam* had made on behalf of the people of Prisma.

While it played, and while the images changed to that of other officials and citizens of Prisma, Votly spirited away to the table where Tara watched silently.

"How did I do?" Votly gasped.

"You shouldn't let the riflemen treat you so harshly," Balt said through a mouthful of gruel.

"I ..." Votly started.

"That rifleman is a moon rock moron," Tara piped in. "Don't pay attention to them, Votly. You've done something really valuable for your crew just now."

Votly's cheeks blushed blue. *How is Tara always so poised and confident?* "Thank you, Tara. How are you after your experience in the gymnasium the other day?"

Tara took a breath. "Things got a little tense after I stormed out after Mallel." Votly and Balt exchanged a glance. "And now he barely even looks at me. It's a shame, because other than that gear-jammed hologram arena, I can't train with anyone. The riflemen aren't an option because that'll cause a riot, the marines are too preoccupied trying to stop everyone from jamming their gears, and Snipes here is too ditzy with his fear of unsteady ground to prove a challenge."

"Hey!" Snipes cut in, still looking pale as the flooring strobed beneath them from the Wave-Form.

Tara ignored him. "Mallel is the only one here I would spar with, but he won't even look at me."

Votly's cheeks blushed blue again. "Spa?" She looked around and leaned in closer. "You mean ... bathe with?"

Tara's laugh surprised her. "No!" she yelled. "I mean to fight, someone to match with."

"Oh, well, Mallel would be a good match, I think ..." Votly's eyes widened. How could she have let the same comment slip by twice? "I mean to fight against, for training."

"But he and I won't get along; it'll turn bloody real fast." Tara sighed. If she noticed Votly's discomfort, she didn't comment on it. "Best not."

Votly nodded, the blue tinge on her peach cheeks fading. "Best not ..."

The messages playing across the screen buzzed and were filled with static; then they were replaced with a high-pitched wail that screamed through the mess hall as the lights flickered and dimmed.

Votly clutched her ears and ducked under the table, and the gathered crew were in an uproar of alarm, rising to their feet as the lights flickered back to working order. The wailing scream died out to a rhythmic drone, and the screen buzzed with dark static.

"Votly." Mallel's voice pierced the din of startled hubbub. "What is that?"

"I don't know." Votly was typing on her holo-pad in frantic fumbles. "There's another signal being picked up from the outer edges of the sun well."

"It's an encrypted signal." Bromean had his own holo-pad out and walked up to the large screen as the rhythmic drone sounded. "That strange sound isn't just void noise or some deranged song from Prisma ... it's a targeted signal."

Mallel looked to Votly with a questioning glance.

Votly shrugged. "He's the communications expert."

Mallel nodded. "Very well. Bromean, I want you to isolate and analyse that signal."

"Yes sir ..." Bromean shuffled out of the room as the mess hall quieted.

"As for the rest of you," Mallel said, "your personal messages have been relayed to your cabins; I suggest you take time to cherish them, because we're passing our home world by. You're dismissed."

Mallel stalked from the room, and Votly noticed Tara's gaze follow him steadily.

Snipes turned back to Flayr to chatter about shooting with a blunderbuss versus a prism rifle, and Tara's eyes flickered back to Votly.

"That wasn't an ordinary signal," Tara said with a steely cold voice.

"How do you know?" Votly asked as the crew milled out behind her.

"My symbioid sent a weird feeling down my neck ..."

"Your Luck Symbioid? Does that mean the signal is good news?"

"No ..." Tara suppressed a shiver. "The *other* symbioid, the one that helped me repel Rella when he tried to take over my body ... It *did not* like that strange song."

Votly nodded and turned back to the now inert screen as it was wound up mechanically towards the ceiling, "I suppose I should give Bromean a hand."

* * *

It was not so simple to just drop everything and help Bromean. With his focus on decrypting the signal, his duties had to be taken on by the support staff on the bridge, which meant mostly Votly.

After the day shift had been filled, Votly left the bridge—massaging weary eyes—and made for the secluded workspace down the hallway. Bromean had been tucked away there since the signal the day before, working diligently. Despite the extra workload his absence caused, it was a relief, because his attitude towards Tara, Snipes, and the captain was starting to wear on her.

She stopped by the sliding doors, her hand hovering over the opening panel. Bromean was not alone in the encryption room. There were harsh whispers ... *An argument?*

Votly stepped back as the doors slid open, and Corporal Keihn stepped out. His shocked expression upon seeing her turned quickly to a derisive sneer. "Well, if it isn't Techie Votly." His face was bruised from his altercation with Tara, and his arm was in a temporary sling from where it had been dislocated.

"Th-that's officer to you, Corporal," Votly squeaked.

Keihn's sneer turned into a snarl as he stepped forward, and Votly nearly squeaked again. "You don't deserve my respect. I still remember that slap, *Techie*. You mark my words, stay out of my way, or there will be trouble."

Votly gulped. "I'm sure the captain would love to hear about your threatening a member of the command crew. Is that what you were doing in there? Threatening poor Bromean?"

Keihn snorted, his bronze cheeks flushing blue. "Bromean knows where his loyalties lie, unlike others." He barged past Votly, knocking into her with his good shoulder before marching down the hallway.

Votly scurried into the encryption room and shut the door behind her with a hurried breath. "What was that shattered fiend doing in here?" Votly asked.

"I just wanted to talk to him about something." Bromean's bronzed skin was sweaty; he wiped his brow and turned from Votly to hunch over his console again.

"About what? The captain should have been the first to know about the signal."

"The signal is just space noise," Bromean muttered. "A signal from a pulsar sun some million light leagues away that just happened to get picked up by our communications equipment."

"I find that very unlikely," Votly tutted. "The odds of us picking that up is one thing, but also it coming from the same direction that we are heading? That's another." *Also*, she thought, *Tara's symbioid did not agree, not that Bromean would trust what Tara had to say ...*

"Unlikely things happen, Votly. For instance, Scrond chose you as his pupil over me."

Votly bit back a gasp. "He ..."

"Will that be all, Officer?" Bromean turned and stared at her sternly.

Votly huffed, "No, Tara's symbioid detected something strange with that signal."

She regretted letting her anger get the better of her. As she said it Bromean's expression instantly hardened. "How can you trust her? She has not one but two scions of the Rel in her."

"Not Rel! Symbioids, a slither of the moon creatures that used to protect us from the cosmos before the Rel got to them. One just grants her good luck; the other was some kind of command nodule from the original Guardian. It was able to repel the Rel. She is an asset, Bromean. We need her. And if her symbioid says this signal is trouble, then maybe it is. The Rel scions that took out our moon and her moon were slightly different; they affected the guardians and our people in slightly different ways. Maybe this signal is also different for the same reason?"

"In that case, leave me be so I can analyse it further, and you can go play with your infected alien friend."

Votly huffed again and stormed from the room.

CHAPTER 4

Tara Star

ara took a deep breath and steadied herself.

She stood with Votly in the cargo hold beneath the rear of the ship—the one that they had leaped from to fight the battle over Copper Cobble. In its side was an airtight compartment with a control panel that Votly was busy typing away at, oblivious to the cargo workers in the bay who kept giving them odd looks.

"They don't seem to be too used to this kind of thing," Tara said, tugging uselessly at her collar—a copper-tinged metal component that an airtight helmet would lock in to.

"They're just wary I'll open the airlock while the ship is in Wave-Form." Votly waved dismissively over her shoulder without looking up from her task. "I'm the highest-ranking technician on this ship; I'm not stupid enough to do that." Her airy voice hesitated as she spoke.

Tara looked up from the thrumming waves of light that pulsed down the cargo hold's flooring and cocked her head at the slight technician. "You don't seem so sure?"

Votly stopped mid-typing and her shoulders sagged. "No one on this ship respects me."

"Why do you need them to?"

Votly spun, her brow furrowed as she retorted, "Because I'm a part of the bridge command crew; they should respect me. If I have to relay orders, no one listens to me unless I say the order came from the captain."

"Because you're a girl?" Tara felt her teeth clenching.

"No, the other women on this ship don't listen to me either, but I have the rank!"

"You still seem unsure." Tara let her jaw relax with a sigh. "A word of advice from someone who once felt the same way ..."

Votly looked up, her amber eyes hopeful.

"The person you need to most respect you is you. Until you do, no one else is going to have a reason to."

Votly sagged again. "How?"

Tara shrugged. "For me, it was necessity. I still struggle, but then I had greater things to worry about." She stepped forward and placed her hand—bulky with the void suit—on Votly's shoulder, and she shifted under the added weight. "You need to realise the value you give to the task at hand, and complete that task even in the face of great adversity. Circumstance may force this, but you must find a way to do it on your own in the meantime."

Votly nodded quietly.

The ship thrummed, and a distorted voice spoke over the audio system warning the crew to brace for leaving Wave-Form. There was a colossal rumble, and the ship rattled in response as the engine ceased and the strobing light waned into nothing.

One of the hold's crew cheered, "Hey, man, we finally matter!"

"Get back to work!" his colleague replied in annoyance.

"Snipes would have hated that." Tara chuckled, stomping on the now solid flooring.

"Where is he, by the way?" Votly asked.

Tara cringed. "He's made a friend with one of the other ladies on the vessel. Her name is Flayr; she's a prism marine. I mean ... the riflemen don't even look at him. I've spent a lot of nights wandering the hallways rather than share a bunk with what's going on in our cabin."

"Yes, Mallel said he noticed you wandering around on the security feeds at night," Votly hummed, before her eyes widened.

Tara stiffened, her mind splitting between two very different reasons Mallel would do that. Either he still didn't trust her ... the tingling of the Luck Symbioid flared ... or ...

"I mean ... so does ..." Votly's eyes darted wildly. "I mean ..." Then they lit up, finding something to change the topic to. "Do our ... I mean with Snipes and Flayr, do our parts match?"

Tara was already going red in the face, but that made her cheeks blush brightly indeed. "I ... haven't asked. But based off his smug grin every morning, I would say that yes, yes, they do."

"Oh …" Votly stood there for a moment longer—a moment too long, Tara thought—before turning back to the panel and opening the interior air lock door.

As they stepped into the tiny compartment, Votly turned to place the encasing helmet over Tara's head to lock in place around her collar. The confining helmet coupled with the already confining air lock uneased Tara, she was struck with a sense of claustrophobia.

"Now I'll be able to speak with you out there through the communications system," Votly explained as she checked over Tara's suit.

"Why would we need that?" Tara asked.

"Because in the void there is no atmosphere out there, silly. No particles for the sound waves to travel on. We translate the sound in our helmets to an electromagnetic wave that can propel through the ether and then it is translated again back into sound through the speakers in your helmet."

"Right …" Tara tried to wrap her head around that, but gave up, instead focusing on a different line of questioning. "So what would happen if the ship's air lock opened in Wave-Form?" Tara tried to take her mind off the claustrophobia as Votly clicked and clacked the collar seals in place, sealing Tara inside with an audible hiss.

"Oh, well, if there is any integrity failing with the Dustmote or the engine's process, well, then we could fractalize, scatter into a billion specks of light and matter all over the stars … or at least until our quantum momentum is stalled enough to slam back into real space. Then we would freeze and explode in the cold vacuum of the void … if we aren't mangled by the whole process before that, that is …"

She stopped speaking, seeing Tara's hardening expression. "Are you about to attack me?"

"No," Tara gritted her teeth, "I am trying to stop my gears from jamming."

"Oh, on your world having jammed gears means you're all worked up, right?" Votly asked.

Tara nodded.

"Oh! Oh sweet baby, don't fret, that isn't going to happen. We've come out of Wave-Form on the edge of the sun well. We will solar sail in real matter towards our destination. It should be hours at most. We won't Wave-Form any time soon. The engines need to cool."

"I see." Tara hefted herself up, and Votly sealed her own helmet in place.

The suits were big, bulky contraptions, like a diver's suit back on Stemcog, only made from Wizard science and brimming with prisms and technological readouts. The only thing that seemed familiar about them compared to the rest of the vessel, Tara thought, was the copper tinging that graced most of the fixtures back home.

"Now," Votly practically brimmed, her voice echoing through the communications system wired into the helmet, "are you ready for your first void walk?"

Tara steeled herself. "Yes."

Votly turned to the outer door, hit a panel, and the whole room hissed with escaping air. Tara tensed but relaxed at a reassuring word from Votly that crackled in the helmet's communication system. Then Votly hit the open sequence, the outer door of the *Motebeam* slid silently open, and Tara's breath caught in her throat.

Votly—and the rest of the Light Wizards—called the space between worlds the void. But it was not a void at all. It was not a deep black chasm of cold nothingness. It was instead a canvas of celestial art.

Beyond the drifting celestial dust that trailed off the hull of the *Motebeam*, the unfiltered beauty of the cosmos spread out before Tara, a deep velvet dark that was sequined with sparkling lights and dyed by nebulous smatterings of colour.

"Whistling steam ..." Tara breathed. "What are those clouds?"

"Mostly gas, ice, and dust." Votly's airy voice crackled over the communications system, and she crossed her arms with her back to the celestial vista, brimming with joy at Tara's awe. "Want to go float about?" She leaned back, tumbling in slow motion out of the gaping air lock.

The stream of dust and ice that cascaded over the *Motebeam's* hull as it tore through the ether was broken by Votly's passing. It was as if she had dashed through the sprinklings of a waterfall, and then it resumed its flow. Tara tentatively reached out with her bulky, copper-gloved fingers and trailed them through the ephemeral stream. She squealed in delight as the dust motes danced around her fingers, reflecting the internal and external light in varying arrays of otherworldly brilliance.

Without another moment's hesitation, Tara dashed from the air lock, and then suddenly felt very ill indeed as the forces of artificial gravity on the ship ceased to act upon her. Her breakfast rose up in her guts, threatening to spill back up her throat and splatter across the innards of her helmet.

But she managed to hold onto her food as she tumbled through the void.

Votly was nearby, pirouetting and frolicking with ease as Tara tried to reorient herself.

"Use the controls on the thumb side of your gloves," Votly instructed. "Don't worry about the *Dustmote* pulling away; our suits are tethered with a resonate force."

"They're what?" Tara asked as she thumbed the little knobs and buttons that ran down the outside of her index finger to the base of her thumb, getting a feel for which of the little thrusters moved her in which direction.

As the *Motebeam* slid under ... over—it was hard to tell out here—from her, she felt a gentle tug as if from a lifeline, keeping her more or less in line with the ship. *So long as it works.*

"How long does our air supply last?" Tara wondered.

"A few hours, less if we're exerting ourselves. Want to go for a ride?" Votly winked.

Tara set her face into a determined smile and nodded. At Votly's word, she unsteadily followed the technician in a spiralling journey over the *Motebeam*. Its sleek chrome hull reflected the celestial canopy brilliantly—save for the parts marred by its battles on Stemcog—as well as reflecting the pulsing amber light from the solar-powered sails that splayed out above it.

With every gasp and every exertion of propulsion from the tiny thrusters around her suit, little gauges below the line of the lens of Tara's helmet dipped and wavered, until the two void swimmers came to rest, dancing above the bridge of the ship.

A large, dark world hung in orbit before them; the *Motebeam* was making a pass beneath it.

"Whatever anomaly we detected," Votly said breathlessly, "it passed behind that planetoid a little before we came out of

Wave-Form. We should be swinging around into view any moment now."

"Shouldn't we be inside then?"

Votly shook her head. "Whatever it is, even from this *close* distance, it'll take a day for either party to reach each other, the same for any weapon to come within harming distance of us. This is as good a place as any to watch."

"Oh." Tara let the silence pass by. As the two bobbed along in the ether, her tingling spiked. She wanted to ask Votly about Mallel ... but instead she decided to ask the question that the Luck Symbioid did not want her to ask.

Good luck for me is bad luck for others, she thought. *I'm not trusting you to help me.* The tingling flared in protest, but Tara ignored it.

"Why does Mallel not trust me?"

Votly rounded on Tara, shocked or alarmed, she could not tell through both her helmet and Votly's.

"Mallel wouldn't have brought you on board if he didn't trust you." Votly crossed her arms.

The tingling flared; Tara decided not to ask the follow-up question. She didn't care for the answer, not if it was what the Luck Symbioid wanted her to know. She bit her lip and swore internally. The tingling started to burn.

Tara found herself shaking, tensing, anything to avoid the sensation that needed to be addressed. She knew what she wanted to ask; she knew what the symbioid was telling her to ask. And that was why she could not. *If you won't leave me*, she threatened, *I'll make this hurt for the both of us. So, be quiet.*

The tingling flared again—so painful that Tara's vision went white—and then subsided.

Good.

Tara needed to take her mind off the internal battle she was waging. "What's that?"

Votly was holding her arm up to the little world that hung before them, tapping on a device in her gauntlet that had lenses flipping up and directing light into a little hologram display.

"This is my wrist-mounted light lab," Votly explained.

Tara looked at it for a good moment. "So ... a Light Gauntlet? Where did you get it?"

"High Prismatist Scrond taught me how to make it ... I was his student."

"Oh, I'm sorry you lost him ..." Tara sagged. "He seemed a good man, and he died completing his goal."

"I know ... it's just ..."

"Just what?"

"It's just that without Scrond, it seems the purpose holding this crew together has waned. The riflemen followed him; they were seconded onto this ship at his behest. Mallel and his marines, well, they never really got on with the riflemen."

"And Scrond was teaching you to be a Wizard like him. I bet he thought this would break the divide between the two factions?"

Votly giggled. "The Wizardry your people saw was his science and knowledge. He was teaching me to be a Prismatist. He was the last of his kind, and now the knowledge of his order is lost forever. I could not learn enough from him in time."

"How much can you do?" Tara asked.

"I learned the science and engineering of manipulating small amounts of light with this contraption here." Votly tapped the gauntlet. "Not much. I'm no Prismatist; I'll never be a Prismatist with such a basic level of knowledge and skill. I'm just a useless techie."

"Maybe not." Tara nodded. "Maybe you can't be a Prismatist, but by doing what you do with light, you could be a Light Wizard."

Votly's giggle was stifled as she considered what Tara had said. "I'm not sure that will be enough to preserve the legacy of my people."

"It will be enough to preserve what you care about," Tara said. "And one day you may rediscover the knowledge that was lost. Hey, if it was discovered once, who's to say you can't discover it again?"

Votly did not answer, but her Light Gauntlet flashed red, rousing them from their discussion. "The anomaly is pulling into view …"

Something was emerging from the other side of the planetoid … something big … something enormous.

The dark shape loomed in the shadow of the world.

"It's …" Votly gasped. "It can't be."

It was as big as the world. Which was impossible. Tara blinked away the disbelief. Something that big could not exist; something that big could not move of its own accord. But here it was.

It was a creature, a titanic beast of unfathomable proportions that emerged from the void, curling around the planet as beams of light from the distant sun lanced across its crown.

It was unimaginable, its great maw dipping down onto the world's surface to scoop up the minerals and ice that clung to its skin. And then the creature ebbed up, propelling itself through the void like a serpent would through water.

"Whistling steam!" Tara cursed. "What in the Three Perversities is that thing?"

The Beast broke off from its feeding of the tiny little world and propelled itself further into the sun well, towards the oncoming path of the *Motebeam*. The flotsam of the world pulled up in its wake to spill out into the ether. It looked like the bottom of a pond had been disturbed by the passing of a great fish, the sediment on the bottom dragging up to muddy the waters in its wake.

Ominous, blaring tones sounded within their suits. The *Motebeam* was sounding the alarm.

* * *

After a harried journey back to the closest air lock, Tara and Votly scrambled to tear off their locked helmets and sprinted in an awkward clunk-thunk manner through the chrome corridors, which were swarming with scurrying Prismath.

Although the void suit was somewhat streamlined and agile compared to the diving suits Tara knew of back on her home world, she still did not like the way she was weighed down by it.

They quickly found themselves on the bridge with most of the command crew. There was Captain Mallel, Bromean, some of the higher-ranking members of the marines—including Balt—and Snipes, who seemed to be more comfortable now that the ship had stopped throbbing with coloured light.

Snipes gave her a nod as she entered, her bangs splayed from her hood since she had quickly thrown the garment over her void suit—it contained most of her smoke bombs and throwing knives. Tara nodded back, pulling her yellow scarf up over her face. If there was going to be a battle, she was going to be ready for it.

Mallel turned at their entrance.

"Votly." His voice was steady, even though his posture was more strained than usual. "Nice of you to join us."

"I slowed her down," Tara said, striding past Mallel to the main view screen across the far wall of the bridge. The Prismath had used their science-wizardry to try to analyse the Beast in the void. A rough schematic of it was superimposed next to an image of the planetoid it had just wrecked in a hologram by the view screen.

The Beast was hard to comprehend. It was like a crevassed, stone-metal whale from someone's nightmare. It was made of metallic-looking segments that ebbed and swayed as it propelled itself forward. Each segment was crested by a tower-like spine protruding from the top and the bottom, with large, splaying fins underneath it like those of a whale. Its snout protruded to form a gigantic maw with razor-sharp teeth that may as well have been the jagged peaks of mountains, and it had an exoskeleton skull that would have struck fear into anyone no matter its size.

Tiny little asteroids orbited around it, trailing behind in its wake.

"How is it moving without thrusters?" Tara asked.

"You catch on quick." Votly beamed as her fingers flew over her console to produce more readouts and data that streamed alongside the superimposed hologram. "Its segments are made of some kind of semi-organic metal ore. Every time it sways, the segments produce an alternating electromagnetic field that propels it forward, much like how light travels through the ether."

"For those of us who aren't wizards?" Snipes coughed.

"It creates its own propelling force by its own movement," Mallel said.

"What about the planets orbiting it?" Tara asked.

"The Beast is so large, it has its own gravitational pull." Votly was sweating, her cheeks flushed with deep blue blood. "Sir, I am detecting evidence of civilisations on those worlds. The ... the Beast is *inhabited!*"

"Rel?" Mallel stepped to look over her shoulder.

"I am detecting negligible traces of the enemy. I can't tell if there is any Rel presence there now, but there definitely was in the past."

"Then this is just a natural creature?" Tara said. "So long as we avoid it, what do we have to fear?"

The entire bridge turned to face her, stunned.

"Look at that thing!" Balt protested.

"Yeah, but people live there." Tara gestured at the asteroids. "I don't see why it should pose a threat so long as we don't provoke it."

"Tara would be right under other circumstances. The aliens on those worlds would live in harmony with the Beast ..." Votly's sweat ran freely down her face. "But trajectories put that thing on a path to Prisma ... Tara, it is as large and more dense than the entire continent you are from back on Stemcog. You saw what it's done feeding on that world. It's a planet killer."

"So the Rel must have altered its course." Tara bit her lip. "We need to somehow alter it back. Perhaps we can make contact with the people who live around it?"

"But that will take time, Tara!" Votly was practically yelling. "My projections estimate it will get to Prisma within days, and then to Stemcog shortly after that."

"How does that work?" Snipes chimed in. "It isn't in Wave-Form."

Votly was skimming her readouts madly. "No, it isn't in Wave-Form, but it has immense mass and is moving with such a great momentum relative to the sun well that it is warping time in the same manner we would while in Wave-Form. Even though we're not travelling right now, we're still close enough to the Beast to feel the effects. Less than three days, from our perspective, that's how long our worlds have."

"Bromean?" Mallel turned to the sweating tech. "Can we make contact with the people living there?"

"I'm detecting multiple key signatures. The people who live there aren't all one people, and they aren't all that friendly to each other. It seems like they've been at war for years based off all the noise I'm detecting."

"That could be interference from the thing itself," Votly countered. "We won't know until we get closer, I am afraid."

The crew now turned to face Mallel. He set his jaw, squeezing the hilt of his energy cutlass. Only Tara noticed his eyes flitter from the screen for a split second, to glance over Scrond's staff—which rested next to the captain's chair—and then to glance over her.

"Set a course for the Beast's skull. Take every precaution available," Mallel ordered.

"Aye, Cap'n," one of the techs said.

"Balt," Mallel turned to the marine, who stood to attention, "prepare our forces for conflict. I want everyone on violet alert."

"Aye." Balt saluted and turned from the bridge, marching out into the chrome-coloured corridors.

"How long until we arrive?" Mallel asked.

The tech behind the helm furrowed her brow. "About a day, Cap'n. I fear it may seem much longer than that."

"So be it."

"What do you intend to do when you get there, Captain?" Tara asked.

The hubbub in the room died down as Mallel and Tara regarded each other. "I think you know what I have to do, Miss Star. You heard Votly; we have three days to save our worlds from that thing." He pointed to the holographic display.

"We can find a way to deflect it," Tara said coldly. "How many people live around that thing do you think? Do you really want to butcher more cities if you don't have to?"

Mallel stiffened. The tension building between the two continued to brim and thicken. "In case it isn't obvious to you Miss Star." The words were drawn from his lips like blood from stone. "But we have a world-sized Beast bearing down upon our homes. And I doubt we have the means to destroy it let alone convince it to move. Anyone with that kind of power would be someone I mistrust very much indeed. Do you have that power?"

Tara's symbioid flared, not her Luck Symbioid ... this was the other one. Instead of a burning tingling, it was like a wave of cool silk enwrapping her spine. She suppressed a shiver. "I guess until we find out, we have no choice but to work with each other again."

She turned from him and stalked out of the bridge.

* * *

The crew of the *Motebeam* spent the passage of time with a sense of foreboding dread. Mallel had been open with the crew about the emergent Beast, sharing the limited information they possessed. The images of the Beast streamed over the viewing screens in the mess, where the noncombat members of the crew found themselves waiting while not on duty.

The atmosphere in the mess was tense, and the Prismath murmured among themselves.

"A little different from SWiGS, eh?" Snipes asked as he polished down his blunderbuss's barrel modification with an oiled cloth.

"SWiGS seemed more manageable." Tara wanted to make a comment about Snipes maintaining his weapon in the mess; it felt like it was rude to their hosts. But she would be a hypocrite for doing so, as her cloak was full of an assortment of knives, smoke bombs, and the like.

"Who knows," Snipes said, "this Beast might be a big softy."

"I killed a big softy once." Tara bit her lip. "He was my first target as a Night Assassin. I poisoned his whisky. Then we fought, and then he offered me a drink ..." She sighed.

A moment later Snipes stopped cleaning his weapon and looked up at her. "You saying we could poison this thing?"

"I'm saying I don't want to kill anything that isn't actively trying to kill us."

"That's very," Snipes paused again, looking up from the polishing of his blunderbuss attachment, "Thomas of you."

Tara smirked. "Perhaps that's why Thomas and I generally got along."

"Hmm." Snipes huffed a dismissive laugh in good faith, and then returned to his polishing. "Mallel is right, though, you know. We may not have a choice."

"We'll see," Tara said, tapping her fingers against the table "We'll see ..."

A klaxon sounded, a harsh piercing sound that jolted the Prismath from their nervous ruminations. Before the tone died down, Tara realised she had jumped back from the table and had a smoke bomb in her hand.

The tone sounded again, and by the time this second one died down, Snipes had slotted the last of his attachments onto his gun and racked the chamber.

"Warning, proximity alert." Votly's voice sounded over the loudspeaker system. "Prepare for imminent engagement. Staff all offensive and defensive stations. Any noncombat personnel are to hunker down."

The message repeated—interspersed by klaxon blaring—as Tara and Snipes surged through the chrome corridors towards the bridge. They dashed past an air lock being barricaded by marines and then passed another air lock where the riflemen sat around idly.

Tara gave Snipes a look as they ran by, but they were rushing past the scurrying personnel to reach the bridge and didn't have time to discuss it.

The bridge door slid open at their arrival; Mallel looked up from his prism pistol, where he was slotting a polished refractor crystal into the clawlike barrel.

"What is it?" Snipes asked.

"Take a position over there, Snipes." Mallel pointed to a large, blockish console in the corner.

The screen behind Mallel flashed with the fire of prism cannons into the void. They were not aiming at the Beast, which was now looming so close, its snout blotted out most of the cosmos. They were firing on an object arching out from beneath it.

Votly was furiously typing away at her console, shouting random bits of technological gibberish as Snipes clambered onto his cramped little roost and took aim at the only logical place, the door to the bridge.

"They keep tracking our vector every time we shift!" Votly cried. "All beams have been deflected thus far!"

"Shouldn't we be setting up elsewhere?" Tara asked. "Why are we reinforcing the bridge?"

Mallel shook his head, drawing his energy cutlass and powering it on. The blade brimmed with crackling energy. "Because this reeks of foul deeds. That ship coming towards us, it shouldn't be avoiding our fire like it is; it's too primitive compared to the *Motebeam*."

"Treason?" Tara blanched.

"The ..." Mallel was cut off as Votly barked more information in a harried manner.

"Their resonance frequency keeps deactivating when we fire, throwing off our telemetry data; then it reorients towards us after evading our salvo!"

"They know our resonance frequency," Tara realised. "But I thought it was specific to the *Motebeam*? That only we know it?"

Mallel's grip was so tight on his pistol and cutlass that his knuckles turned pale. "I know."

The bridge doors slid open, and Bromean hurried in, his uniform half buttoned.

"Where were you, technician?" Mallel demanded.

"I was ensuring the air locks by the bridge were adequately guarded, sir." Bromean hurried to his console.

"So you whipped those riflemen into shape ... the ones by the bow air lock that didn't seem too prepared, right?" Tara asked.

Bromean tensed.

Mallel leaned forward. "Right, technician?"

"Brace for impact!" Votly cried.

The ship rocked as the object hurtling from the gravitational pull of the Beast slammed into the side of the *Motebeam* with a horrid shriek of metal. Lights flickered and went out, pipes burst, spewing steam, or air, or oil.

Mallel stumbled onto his hands and knees in the dark, mindlessly reaching for Tara's sprawled form to see if she was all right. He gripped her leg, and her calf tensed ... She was standing upright.

He glanced up Tara's sleek form, and she glanced back down at him as the lights flickered on, her brow cocked in a questioning gesture. She had not toppled like the rest of the crew.

"You all right, Captain?" There was no reproach in her voice.

Mallel scrambled up onto his feet, blue tinging his dark cheeks. "I thought you might have fallen with the impact." He took a moment to realise they had been struck, and his eyes widened. "Report, what's our status?"

Another of the technicians was hauling himself back into his chair, coughing as he squinted in the dimming light to see. "Hull integrity secure at ninety-eight percent; only small compartments were breached. The enemy collided with us and latched onto an area over the Realyegh air lock."

Tara glanced over at the sprawled form of Bromean as he struggled to shrink into the corner. He was sweating, nervous ... but not fearful.

Tara stalked over to him, drawing a throwing knife and dragging him from the console with a squeak of protest. She placed the knife to his neck hard enough to draw a thin line of blue blood. "Who are these people?"

Bromean's eyes widened and then narrowed in rage within an instant. "What are you implying?"

Tara pressed harder with the knife, and his rage stifled. "Is the Realyegh air lock the one three junctions back from the bridge corridor? The one guarded by the riflemen?"

The stifling rage evaporated, and Bromean bit back a choke. But he managed to rally. "You are touched by the Rel. The ones boarding us seek to rid the Rel influence from this sun well. The riflemen will do the duty that the marines fail to do."

"Bromean!" Votly gasped.

They were distracted by sounds of beam fire outside the bridge, as well as the sound of shrieking metal and screams. Not all of the screams were produced by the Prismath. There was something else on board.

"Are you saying this is a coup?" Snipes was pulling himself back into his roost, training his sights on the door.

"On ships we call it a mutiny." Mallel turned to the marines on the bridge. "We have been betrayed. Prepare to kill our own people," he snarled. "Any armed Prismath wearing the brown is to be treated as hostile. Am I understood, void sailors?"

"Aye, Cap'n!" The chorus came from the small squad in the bridge.

"Votly, warn the rest of the ship."

"Aye." Votly tapped on her console and then spoke the dreadful revelation over the communication system as more shrieks and beam fire sounded from the corridor outside the bridge.

The enemy was drawing closer.

"Their goal will be to overwhelm the bridge and take over this ship, MY SHIP!" Mallel bellowed. "We aren't going to let that happen."

Tara turned back to the trembling Bromean and squeezed his neck so hard, he croaked. "Who are these people that are boarding us? What are they like?"

Bromean smiled. "They are the Slithmet. They dwell on the Beast and wear armour like you've never encountered. Your weapons will be useless! They will tear through you like you tore through us on Stemcog."

Tara hissed and kneed Bromean in the gut. He groaned and collapsed in a heap as she spun and readied herself to stand with Mallel behind the crude barricade being formed by the bridge doors.

"I never wanted to kill your people," Tara spat. "Not after I got up close to you." She pulled her scarf up over her mouth. She still wore it around her neck even with her bulky void helmet on. The visor was slid back for the moment.

"Neither did I." Mallel's voice was hard again, growing colder as his lips were pulled back into a vicious snarl. "When I was a child, when the Rel husked my kin, I had no choice, they had no choice. But these people here turn against us of their own will ... There will be a *reckoning!*"

The doors shuddered with an impact and screeched with rending metal as they were bent inwards by something monstrously strong.

The marines and technicians shied back as the lights flickered and waned.

Mallel and Tara did not.

The rumbling thunder of conflict intensified as other marines surged towards the bridge from outside. But they were kept at bay as the doors were rocked again, warping inwards. Then they were punctured—gripped by something with sharp talons—and peeled back at the corner. The door was breached, and some insidious metallic thing reached through.

Mallel raised his pistol to fire, but a crack from Snipes's rifle had already sounded. The bullet pinged into the creature's hand, and it shrieked and recoiled.

There was a moment of reprieve, and then the door was rocked violently again, and the top was peeled back further. A rifleman in brown peeped over with his beam rifle to fire a pot shot. But a quick throwing knife from Tara had him tumble back with a wet grunt.

Smoke seeped into the room from the breached door, filtering into the ceiling to be siphoned by the venting system.

"They're not going to get in here," Mallel muttered.

But Tara's eyes followed the smoke through the vents ... the same vents that she had snuck through her first time on this ship when it crashed into the Baul Islands. The smoke shifted as it flowed around a serpentine shape in the opening and Tara shuddered.

It looked like something from the horrible tales of the deep, of vicious half-human creatures that would lure men to their deaths with their song and feed upon them. Only this monster was covered in skin of segmented metal, with viciously hooked talons, glowing red eyes, and a batlike face that snarled in a perpetually sadistic smile.

It was a siren of the deep cosmos, a siren of stone and metal.

"Open fire!" Mallel's commanding voice pierced the smoke-choked battle din, and the marines obeyed.

The siren's—the Slithmet's—hard face was chipped by strobing beam fire in the gathering dim. The shots scorched and sizzled pieces of steel-like skin, but the creature lowered itself into the bridge as if unmolested, uncoiling from the venting like a snake, and then it tore the closest marine in half.

Blue blood spattered across the room as the Slithmet tossed the legs at Mallel—knocking him back—and the torso of the still screaming marine at the door as it was wrenched open with a horrendous shriek.

More of the serpentine creatures spilled through the breach as the smog behind them flashed with fire from the embattled Prismath on both sides.

Tara made for the first Slithmet. It reacted to her as quick as lightning, whipping its tail around with a crack to knock the legs from under her. She leaped over the tail with her own frightening agility and slammed a smoke bomb into its face. The dull blast and hiss of smoke was accompanied by a rattling sound as the fragments of the bomb ricocheted within its mouth and throat.

The creature choked and collapsed with a clunk onto the chrome flooring, gagging and spluttering.

Mallel righted himself from his tumble and charged the first interloper; it had coiled around another marine and was squeezing so hard that his bones popped. With his energy cutlass Mallel slashed across the creature's back. Magnetic flakes chipped from its exoskeleton and got caught in the sword's electronic charge, circling the powered cutlass in a spiralling pattern.

With a vicious howl the Slithmet turned on him and bore down to bury its fangs into Mallel's skull.

A quick crack shot from Snipes struck the thing's glowing red eye, and it howled and reared so high that it slammed into the ceiling. The marine in its grip was released with a relieved gasp, and he steeled himself to scramble up the Slithmet's segmented body and jam his rifle into its open maw.

The marine pulled the trigger, and the beam pulse burst through the innards of its head, its eyes flaring with bright colours before it collapsed limply onto the floor.

"They can die!" Mallel barked. "Share this knowledge with them!" He turned onto the breach as his marines barked acknowledgment, realising that it wouldn't do them much good.

Several Slithmet slithered in to wreak havoc on the scattered defences as a squadron of riflemen poured in after them to shoot at the stragglers.

"Traitors!" Mallel charged forward without hesitation, but was pounced upon by one of the Slithmet, which pinned in him place with its cruel talons.

Tara reacted quickly, launching forward to slam her knife into its skull, but it glanced off the almost impervious exoskeleton with a clang.

It looked up, red eyes narrowing in an insidious glare, and it grinned.

"Tara Night," it hissed.

Tara darted back in momentary fright. "My name is Star!" She slammed another bomb into its grinning maw and hook kicked it across the jaw.

This particular bomb was a flash bomb.

The rapid white blast in the churning chaos of the battle disoriented all the combatants.

Tara knew it was a poor tactical move; setting off a flash bomb practically in your own face was a surefire way to get killed in the heat of battle. She only lamented her decision when she felt talons grip her shoulders and haul her across the room on her knees. She was painfully aware of this even as her ears rang and her eyes struggled to focus.

But Mallel was pinned by that thing. She tried to justify her reckless decision. The tingling had suggested another course of action, but she, of course, ignored it. If she took that action, Mallel may still have been in danger. Since she kept rejecting the luck, she assumed the symbioid was just screaming at her to do *something*, but, she also realised, she was still alive. Maybe she could not shake off the Luck Symbioid like she thought.

She blinked through the dizziness, the ringing dulled somewhat, and her eyes focused enough to know that the battle was over. Marines and technicians were being lined up on their knees somewhere behind her; Snipes was slumped in his corner; Votly was screaming as she was pried away from her console; and Tara was brought up to the helm with Mallel. They were on their knees in front of Bromean.

A Slithmet stood over Bromean's shoulder, leering down at its captives with glee. A rifleman carrying a prism pistol with his other arm in a sling rushed in to give Bromean a report and turned to smirk at Tara and Mallel—it was Corporal Keihn.

"We've secured the conduits towards the bridge, Bromean. The marines are still trying to break through, but we're keeping them at bay. The engine room is still putting up resistance; we can't get in."

"Send another squadron and take two of my warriors," the Slithmet said, its voice an insidious metallic hiss. "Tell them not to come back until we have control of the whole ship."

Keihn saluted and ordered a group of his riflemen to leave, followed by two of the slithering Slithmet.

The corporal remained, however, when he saw Votly. "Oh, Votly," he smirked as he marched over to her, pushing her over. "So bad to see you survived!"

Mallel was shouting after him not to touch his crew. Keihn doubled back and struck him across the face, but Tara tuned all of that out. The Slithmet that seemed to be in charge never took its eyes from her.

"Tara," it said. Its metallic leer tried to pierce into her soul, but she resisted quite easily.

"Who are you?" she growled.

"We are but refugees looking to enact revenge against a cruel and indifferent cosmos. We have been told a great deal about the young woman who quelled the Rel Scion ... I expected you to be ... fiercer."

With a snarl Tara wrenched away from the talon gripping her shoulder and kicked the Slithmet's face savagely. It flinched under the blow but remained mostly unperturbed.

"Is that fierce enough for you, monster!" she cried. "The cosmos won't give a gear-jammed cog about your revenge if it's indifferent! Who are you? What do you want with us?"

"And why have you sided with turncoats!" Mallel's voice was low, but the weight behind it could have sunk an island.

"These things fight the Rel as we do," Bromean answered. "But you, Captain, have let someone onto our ship who not only killed our friends, but had the Rel's barbs hooked into her flesh! She's the enemy, Mallel, and you couldn't see it as you were blinded by your infatuation with her!"

"Bromean, your mind must have been shattered to shards!" Votly screamed from the line of prisoners behind them. "How many of your own people were killed in this mutiny of yours? How do you even know you can trust these creatures?"

"That song we heard on the broadcasts, Votly, it was them." Bromean pointed. "These people have fought a war against the tyrants who live on that Beast for centuries. They know how to stop it; they just need help to get inside its skull ... and in return they'll help us get rid of a captain who lets enemies into our midst."

"You're a shattered fool," Mallel spat. "The blood of the Prismath you killed today will stain your hands forever."

"Less blood than would have been spilled under your leadership." Keihn stepped forward and drew his energy knife. He placed the un-powered blade up to Mallel's throat. The cool, inert steel pressed into Mallel's skin, and if it was ignited, it would render his arteries into oblivion. "These creatures needed our help; the Rel is infecting that Beast's mind!" He gestured to the display of the great, titanic Beast as the *Motebeam* bore closer, its infinite maw taking up the whole screen. "They said with our Wave-Form technology they can get into the skull before the Rel takes full control of it, and they will save the people who orbit around it and live under tyrants! We're following our mission to the letter; we're just removing an obstacle."

Mallel did not reply. Instead he looked up into Keihn's eyes with malice.

"Hmmm," the Slithmet hissed, "how does this Wave-Form engine work?"

Votly squeaked.

The Slithmet homed in on her. "Bring her to me."

Tara struggled under the grip of her captors, snarling as she tried to lash out, but it was in vain. The talons that dug into her were strong, tempered by the chaos of the vacuum and pointed into scythe-like grips that kept her down.

The Slithmet leader gripped Votly by the jaw, its talons drawing blue blood from her flesh. Mallel continued to watch stoically, his eyes burning with something beyond fury.

"Is this the one?" it said.

"She's the one who can control the Wave-Form engine," Bromean said.

"There are many on this ship who can!" Mallel's fury burst forth. "Pick on someone else!"

The Slithmet turned its sinister leer towards the captain, a deadly chuckle grinding in its metal-like throat. "Oh, my dear captain, your outburst is exactly the reason we want this frail thing to do the deed … such a naïve-looking thing." Its eyes flashed bright red, interlaced with layers and layers of black, bloodshot barbs.

Tara stiffened, and the tingling flared with her. Not the tingling of luck, but of the *other* symbioid that was woven with her—the Master Symbioid. It detected the foul presence that was woven in the Slithmet's eyes.

"Mallel," she breathed, "these creatures are husked by the enemy."

Keihn stepped forward and backhanded her across the face. "You would like to convince us of that, wouldn't you? Pathetic. If they were husks, they would be shambling morons just like the ones we've fought before."

Mallel's jaw clenched. "Corporal, when I get out of here, I am going to skin your eyelids."

"Well, aren't you tough, glaring up at me from your knees like that. Don't you like it when I hit your Stemcog wench?" Keihn made to strike Tara again.

"Corporal," Tara gasped. The tingling flared, forcing her to speak even though she tried to suppress it. "Think. These creatures aren't like you or me. Maybe the Rel interacts with them differently?"

Keihn snorted and struck her again.

"I'll do it!" Votly squeaked. "Just don't hurt any of them!"

The Slithmet's grin widened, and rows of sharp, jagged, stone-like teeth gritted against each other with the horrid gesture. "It seems our compatriots were right. This woman was the thing to break."

Sounds of beam fire down the hallways caught its attention. "Prismath, would you and your men deal with that? You know these hallways better than we do."

Keihn seemed conflicted, looking between Bromean and the Slithmet. But at Bromean's nervous nod, Keihn bolted from the bridge, followed by his other riflemen, leaving only the Slithmet to watch over the prisoners ... and Bromean.

"That's an interesting trick," the Slithmet hissed as it watched Keihn and his men filter down the corridor, "that your Symdian companion has."

Bromean cocked his head. "How do you know ..."

The Slithmet slashed Bromean's neck with a deft swipe from its talons.

Shocked pain and bewilderment spread across the paling Prismath's face as his blue life force spurt across the deck. The captured marines and technicians flinched or screamed, but Mallel and Tara remained steadfast.

"Yes, Tara Star ..." it grinned, "we *are* aligned with the Rel. That Great One tore through our world and dragged my people along in its wake. We fought for our new place in the void, attached to the path of that thing like a parasite. But we were repelled by the other inhabitants who live on those worlds.

"The Rel—seeking revenge against your kind—tried to take over its mind through its nerves. But its guardians, the Custanguin, repelled the Rel. But from that battle, the Custanguin are now weakened. So together with the Rel, we can overthrow them, infiltrate the skull, and overwhelm the defenders. Then we can take our revenge on the Great One and its people. We can rule it from the brain stem with righteous might. Then we can turn it on your worlds for the evils you have inflicted upon the Rel's kind."

"You fool," Tara said. "If it were able, the Rel would have taken over your very mind. The fact that it can't is only a small mercy, for it will eventually betray you in other ways."

The Slithmet grinned. "I suppose you would say that. Being weaved with other creatures yourself, you would know *all* about it. Tell me, Tara, did you consent to having your body woven with ... what does your kind call them ... symbioids?"

Tara hesitated.

"I didn't think so." The Slithmet chuckled. "Maybe the Rel isn't the evil you think it is."

"Give it time," Mallel spat. "You'll eat your words."

"We'll see." It turned back to Votly, who was still trapped in its vise-like grip. "Now, little thing, you see what I do to creatures who are of no use to me." It glanced at Bromean's corpse and then pressed its wide head into Votly's. She shrunk as much as its grip would allow. Without taking its head from her, it pointed with blue-dripping talons to the display, to the Beast that now filled the screen. "Ram this ship into that thing's skull, in Wave-Form, now."

Votly squeaked, "But we'll die!"

"You might, but you definitely will if you don't do what I say." It dragged a talon across her cheek, not deep enough to break her flesh ... much.

Tara made fleeting eye contact with Votly, trying to make some communication, but what she saw left her stunned. Beneath Votly's external nerves, her eyes communicated to Tara a focus, a resolve, something Votly did not expect herself, Tara presumed.

What was it Votly had said earlier? Tara's mind raced with the tingling of the Luck Symbioid rising within her. *Something about the Wave-Form engine needing to cool?*

She then glanced to Snipes's slumped form in the corner; the scope glinted in the strobing lights. Tara hoped against hope, ignoring the tingling of the Luck Symbioid, and gave a small, imperceptible nod. The scope didn't move ...

Votly was pressed against the helm with trembling hands as she typed commands, and the ship hummed and pulsed and vibrated as the Wave-Form engine brimmed back to life. Warning images flashed across the display, foretelling of imminent collision—Tara assumed—and advising course correction, but Votly superseded them all.

"How long until we ram into the skull?" the Slithmet said.

Votly's hands stopped shaking as she turned to look into the creature's eyes. "That depends entirely on how long it will take for the engine to warm up. As we didn't have enough time to vent the heat from our last voyage, it won't take too long ... but I wager the *Dustmote* may blow up first."

The Slithmet started. "What?"

Votly shrunk under its voice, but a defiant smirk returned to her face. Tara tensed, sensing her time was close as the Slithmet who gripped her flinched at the news.

"Careful what you wish for," Votly spat.

The Slithmet swiped out with its talons, but a crack shot from Snipes's slumped form rang out. A spray of flechette rounds erupted from his rifle and smashed into the Slithmet's face, shattering its cheek and jaw. The creature reared back with a roar—dropping Votly in its shock—as the marines who were captured took advantage of the sudden confusion and rebelled against their captors.

Votly spun away into the din as Tara jabbed one of her dozens of wrist-concealed throwing knives into the knuckles of the creature that held her down. It shrieked back with a haunting cry, and Tara leaped up into the lead Slithmet, slamming her boot into its cracked temple.

With a sickening snap and a dull, throbbing pain that shot up her leg, the Slithmet lurched away from her. Tara landed bodily on her back. The creature whose knuckles she had jabbed rose onto its coiled tail to slam its considerable jagged mass into her exposed, prone form.

In a flash of crackling energy, Mallel was there, ignited cutlass in hand. He threw his body over Tara's and held his cutlass tip up. As the Slithmet embedded itself onto the crackling, charged tip, it buzzed and vibrated against the metallic exoskeleton of the half-humanoid beast. A straight thrust would not have been enough to penetrate such otherworldly plate, but with its body weight crashing down upon the blade and Mallel's dogged refusal to buck under the same force, the plate cracked open. The blade seeped into the Slithmet's soft interior body as it collapsed onto them.

Tara and Mallel both helped each other to haul the beast from them.

Quietly, with short breaths, she gripped Mallel's shoulders before they could stand again. "Appreciated, Captain," she said.

Mallel nodded, holding her gaze with a hint of ... something, before springing into the fore. He slammed the edge of his cutlass against the lead Slithmet with many a slash and cut and dodge and parry. Its plating chipped away under his barrage, and Tara sprinted, sliding around Mallel's back leg and flinging a throwing knife into their enemy's face to keep it distracted.

Snipes continued to lay down his covering fire. He shot destructive swathes with his flechette rounds, aiming for the sections of mad brawl where the marines were being overwhelmed by their anatomically superior foe.

Even with his help, even with the ferocious zeal that the marines defended their betrayed ship with ... the brawl danced in circles across the deck, with no clear winner revealing themselves any time soon. Despite the advantages these space sirens had over Tara, Snipes, and the crew, they did not have the numbers to win a fight like this without the help of the riflemen.

Perhaps with more time, the crew—aided by the two members of the Symbicate—would have gained the upper hand. Perhaps with time, the prism marines throughout the ship would have overwhelmed the riflemen and breached the bridge to wreak terrible vengeance.

But the ship continued to thrum and pulse. The deck throbbed in bright, colourful lights beneath their feet as the ship carried on in its uninterrupted path into the Beast's maw.

The humming crescendo built, drowning out the shrieks and grunts and pings of metal against exoskeleton. The hum drowned out Tara's battle cry as she leaped and jammed a knife into the lead Slithmet's breastplate, and then Mallel struck at the dislocating segment from below.

Votly dragged herself on her hands and knees to the helm under the din and haze of battle. Slithmet tried to claw at her but were repelled by more expert shots from Snipes. She reached up to the helm. Her trembling fingers reached for the cancel command as the Beast opened its maw wide to swallow the insignificant morsel before it.

As the Wave-Form engine ignited, Votly hit the button.

Tara and Mallel were in a vicious grapple. Sharp talons and a segmented tail glanced off their armour and void suits as they struck back relentlessly in turn. Their bodies brightened, turning to pure Wave-Form and siphoning from their awareness as the *Motebeam* sprung forward, propelled by a half-exploding drive into a mass energy composite—not quite matter, not quite light—and slammed into the Beast's maw. Rows of gargantuan teeth were obliterated before the streak of coloured light slammed into the top of the Beast's mouth and cracked its skull.

The white snap beam shot of the ship then scattered across the innards of the Beast's strange hide, rainbow spectral beams ricocheting in all directions, bent around by the magnetic nature of the beast and catapulted across, through, and around its body to the surrounding satellites.

The searing pain in Tara's eyes subsided as her vision clawed its way back into her consciousness. Somehow her visor had clicked down—an automatic feature, she was sure—with the gauges and indicators below the rim blaring signals that did not seem safe.

She found herself upon a rocky heath, the night sky spread far across the horizon—a sheer contrast to the confined space of the *Motebeam*.

Uneasily she shifted up. Bits of dirt and rock fell from her in swirling patterns before being carried away by misty currents over the surface of the steel-coloured, chalky ground.

She realised quickly that the mist that clung to the surface was not mist, but a layer of floating rock and dust, hovering and twirling in the magnetic eddies of the land she now found herself in. With a groan she struggled further onto her feet … then froze.

Across the horizon a colossal wave of stone and metal emerged, and she quailed in fear.

It was the Beast's tail ... It took her a moment to realise she stood upon on a world that orbited it. She had been scattered by the malfunctioning Wave-Form, flung far from the rest of the crew.

She spun, taking in the desolate world she now found herself on—alone.

"Cogrust!" was all she managed to say.

CHAPTER 5

Tara Star

Tara paced the grey, soiled world in a state of erratic vexation. She stopped and looked up at the gargantuan space Beast as it swam through the void. She looked down, paced some more, and looked back up at the enormous Beast ...

One more time ...

She paced again and looked up, again. "Cogrust!" *I was hoping I was hallucinating,* she thought. *Where in the Three Perversities am I?*

As catastrophically situated as she was, the place possessed an ethereal if harsh beauty. The grey scale world shone with spackled metallic dust, and the undulating tail of the Beast as it rose and fell over the horizon was silhouetted by the majestic tapestry of the cosmos.

Tara slumped onto the rocky ground and crossed her arms; she wasn't in any immediate danger ... or so she hoped. None of those metal siren Slithmet creatures were around, nor were any of the traitor riflemen ... but nor was Mallel, Votly, Snipes, or any of the marines.

"They said there were people on these ..." She was talking aloud to herself in order to assay her brimming panic. The fact that she could not remember the term the Wizards used made her stupidly anxious, given the circumstances. "... worlds," she used in place of the word *satellite*. "If I find some civilisation, maybe I can find Snipes, the Wizards ... Mallel."

She shut her eyes, wishing away the image of Mallel embroiled in the talons of the Slithmet—her tingling flared. The Luck Symbioid was trying to urge some feeling, some comfort, but Tara spat a curse, and it shrunk from her awareness.

The gauge beneath the rim of her visor was blinking; the air metre was dwindling into the red-marked territory. "Well then," she said in a matter-of-fact manner, "best get a move on."

She pulled her hood up over the bulky void helmet—as she was wearing her coat around the suit—and marched across the surface of the world, through the drifting metallic mists that danced in pirouetting eddies around her legs.

The tingling spiked every time her eyes drifted to the depleting air metre within her helmet. She couldn't tell if the Luck Symbioid was trying to tell her something about her air supply or if it was indicating that she might be going in the right direction.

She hesitated, thinking on the situation, but then remembered her promise to ignore the tidings of luck that the symbioid would bring. "Ah, I don't want to rely on you!" She gritted her teeth. "But I'd be a moon rock moron to die out here because I was stubborn. Gear jam you!"

She clenched her fists and stalked through the flotsam of magnetic rock that hovered over the ground. Granules of metallic sand skittered out of her path only to circle around her copper-encased legs in concentric patterns.

Every breath rasped against the inside of her helmet, causing the gauge needle to waver and tilt ever more into the red territory. Tara's rasping became more frequent the more the needle wavered, rising with her panic as her air supply dwindled.

The world she found herself on was a maze of jagged rock, her path winding around alien-looking structures of metal and stone-like shards, over loose granules of black soil, and across silvery veins of some deposit. Every so often a hiss would sound from a crevice in the ground, accompanied by an exhalation of yellow-hued gas. Every time the hissing spew of gasses emerged, Tara had to stop herself from jumping at the noise, and had to bite down hard to stop the Luck Symbioid from tingling. It was desperately trying to tell her something, yet she ignored it.

She rounded a boulder as one of the hissing fissures spewed into her face. She swiped the gas away to clear her vision and found the leering face of a Slithmet.

"Cogrust!" Tara leaped back and drew her knife, ready to fight, ready to kill. But as her breath rasped and misted her visor from within, she realised that this Slithmet was dead.

It sat within a crater with broken arms like gnarled tree branches in the winter; its jaw hung dislocated and sported jagged, broken fangs; and its red eyes were sunken sockets in its metal-like skull plate. Its chest was ripped open, its insides hollow and sparking wanly as its limp tail lolled across the gravel. The thing still looked menacing even in its death, sprawled upon a boulder and half enshrouded in magnetic mists.

Tara took a deep breath to steady her nerves and realised this mangled corpse was the Slithmet she and Mallel had been battling on the *Motebeam*; its cheek and jaw were shattered from where Snipes had shot it. The vile fiend had seen better days. Backing away slowly from the husk of the Slithmet, she continued on her aimless journey.

Eventually, after what was probably twenty minutes—but Tara now considered time in terms of how far the air gauge had tipped into empty—she heard something over the next ridge.

It was a call for help followed by a jeering cry.

That sound was something she recognised in this alien landscape: someone was getting robbed by bandits. She also had a strange thought at that time, one so odd that the tingling of the Luck Symbioid subsided as if in relief. *I thought Votly said you couldn't hear things out in the void?* Tara's thought was dismissed, though, as the cry for help sounded again.

She reached into the folds of her jacket and produced a throwing knife, which she gripped underhanded. She hoped that the bandits were not the same kind of creature as the Slithmet, because by herself she would be next to useless in the coming fight. She sped up a slanted boulder towards where the ruckus was taking place.

She also realised—stupidly—that she could hear crunching underfoot as she moved—another question for later. *Perhaps Votly was wrong?* She dismissed that thought as quickly as she dismissed the returned tingling from the symbioid.

She dashed up the ridge as her raspy breathing grated against her ears, and peeked over the edge. Her breath caught in her throat.

Down the ridge was a frail-looking old man—or alien, as Votly would call it—being harassed by three other aliens just as distinct from him as she was.

He was a withered, knotted thing of twisting grey, wiry flesh, wormlike in nature with thin limbs that sported dull talons. He was hunched over a makeshift cane, with ragged white hair spilling down his gaunt flesh, and was clothed in what looked like worn leather rags.

The things harassing him were kids—punks more like— but they were big and burly, standing a foot taller than Tara. Together they formed a ring around the poor, gangly creature, shoving him and taunting him with derisive sneers.

"What are you going to do?" the leader of the gang snarled. "You don't have no big body!"

I can understand them? Tara realised. *Another question for later.* The Luck Symbioid spiked its tingling, a warning not to leap out like she had planned to do.

So she ignored it.

"Hey!" She leaped over the ridge and skidded down the incline towards the trio gang, who rounded on her with gasps.

The punks were all torso, with rounded bodies and big, bulging eyes struggling to protrude from their hardened masses.

"This ain't none of your business ... whatever you are," the leader said.

"Don't you take that tone with me!" Tara hissed.

The aliens squared up, towering over her, but they seemed so young. She had to figure out how to intimidate them rather than kill them. Deciding to make a show, she flourished her throwing knife in her bulky gloved fingers. But she was less dexterous than she was used to with her suit on, and the knife clattered out of her fingers and dropped into the magnetic eddies of the odd metallic mist that clung to her ankles.

The alien youths eyed one another—and quickly burst out into rolling laughter.

"Moon rock moron!" Tara chastised herself, gritted her teeth, and leaped into action.

Her first kick slammed in between the bulging eyes of the head bully—propelled by the fury of embarrassment. She flipped back after her heel dug into his skin and something cartilage-like cracked. Tara landed in the metallic fog and crouched low as the granules and currents flowed over her void suit, and she was partially concealed in the confusion.

"Ow, my cragulin!" The bully stumbled back, clutching his ... well ... clutching his cragulin—whatever in the Three Perversities that was, and Tara sped to the next one.

She moved low and swift while drawing another knife. She slashed at the toes of the next bully, and with a startled cry, he tried to hop up on one foot, but instead rolled over and tumbled to the ground.

The third one hopped back as Tara rose from the magnetic mists. "You stay back, you!"

"Or what?" Tara hissed and hopped forward—she considered flourishing the knife again, but thought better of it—and said, "Boo!"

"Ah!" The alien turned and ambled away, the other two picking themselves up and hobbling after their companion in the manner of frightened children.

"I hope I didn't hurt them too much," Tara rasped. Her oxygen gauge was dwindling faster with each exertion. The Luck Symbioid was practically screaming at her to take some kind of action, but she stubbornly ignored it. *I won't have another Regen.*

She turned to the old man who was trying to stand upon two gangly legs which protruded from a curve in his wormlike body. This close, he looked decrepit, with short, stubby arms and legs, and dull red eyes. He was roughly the size of a malnourished teenager.

"Are you all right, sir?" Tara hobbled forward; her oxygen gauge was emitting a beeping sound that was steadily creeping up in pitch.

"This really ruined my day ..." His voice was like knotted silk. It had a smooth quality to it, slippery, but every so often it was punctuated by a gravelly sound. "I was supposed to ... Ah well, it doesn't matter anymore. Thank you for helping me, I suppose, miss ..." He turned to Tara, and shock danced across his angular features. His eyes darted from her to her knife and back. He composed himself quickly, his eyes focusing on her helmet. "... What are you?" His voice had a subtly sly quality about it now, but Tara was too preoccupied to notice.

"I'm a mess," Tara said without mirth, her breaths coming short. "The name is Tara."

"Well, Tara, you may call me Hoztic. I am in your debt. And seeing as my ride is destroyed ..." He paused.

Tara scanned the barren, rocky landscape as she struggled to draw a breath. "Your ride?"

Hoztic's eyes flickered for a moment, rolling back in his head like a window shutter before he composed himself. "Yes, those hoodlums threw it down a fissure."

"Oh?" was all Tara could manage. The warning beep was incessant.

"Yes ..." Hoztic answered. "I suppose you'll be heading into town. May I escort you? I would feel better with you around if those hoodlums came back."

"Of course." Tara collapsed onto her knees, gripping her throat.

"Are ... are you all right?" Hoztic peered in through Tara's visor.

"I just don't think I'll make it that far ..." The oxygen gauge tipped into the red. Tara's lungs burned, and her vision danced with exploding stars. She instinctively reached for the helmet clasp—her tingling intensified—and she halted herself. *No!*

"Here." Hoztic gripped her helmet with his stubby hands and started unlatching it.

"No!" Tara said weakly, but she was too deprived of oxygen, and she could not resist.

The helmet hissed, and sweet, fresh air rushed to fill Tara's lungs as Hoztic peeled back the visor. Tara coughed and gasped in astonishment. "There's air here?"

"Of course. How do you think you can hear me?" Hoztic wondered. "How do you think I can breathe?"

The tingling was still flaring in an *I told you so* manner, and Tara's cheeks grew bright red. A small portion of the flaring was trying to bring her attention to something else, the strange opening in the Slithmet's body she had found earlier, the inert eyes that were once shining red, and Hoztic's dull, darting eyes.

"Are you sure you're all right?" Hoztic asked as Tara caught her breath and tried to jam down on the tingling that was almost causing her to writhe. "I *really* need you to protect me right now."

"Yes, yes, I'm fine. You said there's a town around here?" She stood up and patted the granules of dust from her coat.

"Yes … shall we?" Hoztic gestured, a wry expression plastered across his face.

"We shall." Tara nodded. "I need to find a place to regroup."

"I need to regroup with my people as well. I was in an accident, you see." His eyes flickered back in the direction Tara had come from. "Things have not gone as they should have. But I know just the place to make things right."

"Then, Hoztic," Tara said, "lead the way."

CHAPTER 6

Snipes

It was perhaps one of the worst things that could have happened. One minute you're there entangled in a close-quarters brawl with impenetrable space monsters—which, sure, isn't ideal. But then the next moment you are propelled through that cogrusted Wave-Form sorcery, and the next thing you know is that you're being scattered across space.

Or, so it felt.

Snipes was vaguely aware of his body fracturing along wavelengths of light. He was then acutely aware of it shimmering through the nether between particles before the wavelengths ricocheted back into one another to collapse, coughing and spluttering upon sodden ground.

"Whistling steam!" He spat blood and reached for his modified blunderbuss, clutching at more damp ... *something*. "Where am I?"

As far as he could tell, he was in a cave.

He could tell this because it was illuminated.

What it was illuminated by could only be described as a throbbing, celestial light.

It was reminiscent of the pulsing floor of the *Motebeam* as it travelled through Wave-Form, only he was certain this was not the *Motebeam*. For starters, he didn't feel like he was going to throw up ... aside from the whole exploding ship thing. And secondly, he was certain that the *Motebeam* wasn't damp and titanic.

He was starting to get a *really* bad feeling and forced himself to focus through the disorientation.

Echoes and rumblings crawled into his ringing ear canals, describing to him a cavern of vast depth, mass, and movement. The light that rhythmically lit the space was blue and bright, strobing in and out of existence from one end of the cave to the other. It pulsed along curved walls which reeked of metallic lustre and organic sinew.

"Am ..." Snipes struggled to comprehend where he might be, sinking a touch into a damp depression of straining muscle, moisture, and tissue, "... am I *inside* the giant void Beast?"

"Snipes!" A familiar voice rasped from across the undulating cave-scape ...

Oh yeah, Snipes thought with a dreadful horror. *The ground is definitely moving.* The motion was like that of rocking, like a small tugboat summiting and descending the peaks of immense waves in the middle of a hurricane. *I'm going to be sick.*

Snipes's cheeks bulged as he tried to suppress the urge to vomit, only for his efforts to be distracted by the same voice calling out to him. "Snipes, you crooked fool, take cover!"

Snipes looked up as the fresh sick spilled from his mouth, and he saw Flayr of all people propped up against a jutting skeletal structure that could have been described as a boulder.

"What ..." Snipes's questions trailed off as the telltale glint of a rifle scope in the shifting light flickered across his vision, and he dived for a ridge.

A beam from a prism rifle sizzled the muscle sinew near Snipes.

"Come on, you Stemcog bastard!" another voice called—the shooter. "Poke your little head out, and I'll make you feel better after throwing up all over the place!"

"Flayr," Snipes coughed out vomit and rasped, "un-jam my gears and tell me we aren't inside the monster. And tell me we aren't pinned down by one of your rebellious comrades, and please, please, for the love of all that is good in this ... place ... tell me that isn't my blunderbuss out in the open."

"There are a lot of things that I wish I could do right now, dear Snipes ..." Flayr grimaced. "But I cannot do any of that in good conscience and still call myself an honest sailor."

Snipes smacked his head against his cover. "Cogrust!" He then regretted hitting his head against what was, in essence, metallic bone. He bit his lip and scanned the surrounding area, Hired Hero training kicking into gear. "What are our assets?"

"Your wits, my tenacity, and these metallic, skeletal rocks we're hiding behind."

Snipes cursed, a bout of wooziness overcoming him for a moment as the ground shifted with a fresh wave-like movement. "What of our liabilities?"

"Snipes, we are in all kinds of trouble here ... The rifleman pinged my shoulder before I could get to cover. And I think he's got a few buddies moving around one of the crevices to flank us. I'm hurt pretty bad; there's a lot of blood."

Snipes sighed and drew both of his revolver pistols. "Well, no one said gallivanting across the universe to fight evil monsters would be easy. We need to force the rifleman to break cover before his friends flank us. Can you draw his fire?"

"Aye, maybe ..." Flayr did not sound so sure. Her voice was losing its vibrancy. She needed medical attention immediately.

"Well, you do that then. I will break and make for my gun. We should be able to move up that ridge on your left without the blighter taking any accurate shots at us, and we can hold out against his buddies ... You ready?"

Flayr gripped her prism rifle weakly. Inky blood flowed down the barrel and tarnished the prism set into the muzzle. She gritted her teeth and nodded. "I'm ready."

Snipes took a breath and gripped his pistols, pulling the hammers back and relishing the reassuring *click-click* as the cylinders primed to fire their first shots. "Now!"

Flayr screamed as she pulled herself over cover and fired wildly at the metallic ridge where the rifleman was waiting. The rifleman fired a quick beam in response, but it sizzled off Flayr's cover as she ducked back to safety. Snipes took his moment and charged out from cover himself. He fired wildly with his six shooters, making the rifleman curse and duck back into cover as Snipes reached his blunderbuss.

The Beast ebbed again as it moved through space, and Snipes wobbled off-kilter, stumbling to the side and skidding across the ground while missing the blunderbuss completely.

The rifleman recovered and strafed the area with laser fire. Snipes scrambled on his hands and knees while cursing until he reached Flayr's cover.

"Try again, you pounces!" the rifleman taunted. "I've got three more shots left in this prism. You just try again!"

"This isn't going so well." Flayr grimaced.

"No," Snipes panted, "but that moon rock moron just showed us his hand. He only has three shots left."

"Yeah, but his mates ..." Flayr protested.

"It doesn't matter, look; he's not the best shot. He panics easily and has zero discipline ... We can make a move before his friends ..." Snipes trailed off as a scrambling sound behind them made him turn.

In the dulling dark of the rhythmic strobing light, glints from the rectangular goggles of the Wizards' helmets died into dimness. The lights in their prism rifles remained glowing in the gloom and highlighted the riflemen against the alien landscape.

Snipes raised his pistols and fired as he leaped headfirst towards them. The first shot shattered through a rifleman's goggle lens, and he slumped back without time to cry out. The other two ducked, but Snipes was already tumbling over the ridge and engaging in close-quarters combat.

With a pistol whip, Snipes bludgeoned one rifleman while tumbling into the second, and they collapsed in a heap. The bludgeoned man stumbled back with a grunt, gripping his head as he stumbled over the uneven ground, while Snipes became locked in a vicious wrestling match with the other one. Both were trying desperately to gain the upper hand.

Unfortunately, as it went, his opponent gained the upper hand.

He pinned Snipes in place and pulled out one of those energy bristling daggers. The rifleman ignited it, and it hummed with power—only for the rifleman to gasp as the knife was torn from his hand to cling to the nearest protruding boulder with a high-pitched *ring*.

Snipes took the opportunity and thrust one of his pistols up to fire. The rifleman ducked back from the gunshot—forfeiting his pinning position—and Snipes managed to shift and rock the man from him. He stumbled up as the rifleman produced a prism pistol and fired wildly, missing Snipes by mere inches as he retreated over the ridge to where Flayr was dragging herself over to try to help.

"Didn't go so well?" Flayr said with a grimace as Snipes collapsed next to her, each of his pistols scanning the ridge for signs of the rifleman's movements.

"Shut up," Snipes spat, "and get ready."

A device sailed over the ridge and landed before Snipes and Flayr. They both looked at it and blinked. They both spoke at once.

"What's that?" Snipes said.

"Light blast!" Flayr warned.

The world was lit in brilliant white light, and Snipes and Flayr were blinded for seconds. Snipes fired wildly, knowing that the two nearby riflemen would be charging over the ridge to capitalise on their blindness.

One swore and collapsed on the ground somewhere before him.

Flayr's prism rifle also pinged as it fired blindly, and the other rifleman cried out when it hit something.

Snipes scrambled back, firing one pistol while he kept his other hand on Flayr, who half crawled and was half dragged along with him. They both fired with their free hands all the while until their backs pressed up against the same boulder where they found themselves a moment before.

Blinking through the backlit blindness until his vision returned, Snipes came to the groggy realisation that one of the two flanking attackers was dead. He was shot down by Flayr's blind fire. The other was sprawled out on the ground, clawing for his weapon as he was dragged backwards by something pink and gooey.

"What's that?" Snipes huffed.

"Beats me," Flayr wheezed.

"Help me, you bastards!" the rifleman begged as the pink goo wrapped tightly around his leg and dragged him further over the edge of the ridge.

Several competing instincts collided in Snipes's brain: Help the poor man; let whatever was attacking him finish him off; shoot the man dead to save him whatever horrible fate was awaiting him; dive for his own shooter out in the open while the man who had pinned them beforehand was hopefully relocating ...

"Ah," Flayr said, "there's more of that pink stuff!"

Snipes's decision process was interrupted as more of the pink, gooey substance seeped from the sinew and skeletal structure around them. It pawed at their limbs with feeling white tendrils and threatened to ensnare them as it had the poor rifleman, who was being dragged screaming into another crevice.

"I don't want to wait around to find out what it's going to do to us." Snipes hopped up while ejecting his revolver cylinders and locking in fresh ones. He pulled Flayr onto her feet by the scruff of her neck, and they ran out of the seeking, gooey tendrils as if running out of knee-deep mud, heading for Snipes's blunderbuss, which lay on the ground.

The goo was pooling around it too, enshrouding it before pulling it away.

"Cogrust!" Snipes shuffled away from his lost weapon and across the open terrain, towards a skeletal, rocky-looking cliff structure that was lit forebodingly by the strobing light.

"Hey, hey, you two! Don't leave me here!" The shooter who had pinned them earlier bolted from his own cover, ripping away from a limb of pink goo that was pawing at his coat.

Snipes turned and raised his pistol at the shooter, who stopped dead in his tracks.

"You wouldn't shoot me like this, would you?" the rifleman asked, desperate terror saturating his voice.

Snipes pulled the trigger. The bullet impacted a thicker limb that was about to wrap itself around the rifleman's foot. The goo retreated with a rumbling sound that could have been a roar.

"Unless you want me to shoot you, you'll head through here first!" Snipes warned, gesturing to a cave in the cliff-like formation.

The rifleman looked dubiously from Snipes, to Flayr, to the deep, dark cave. The pink goo emerged with another rumbling roar behind him. It surged out of the cracks and pores around them and pooled into a large, globular monster. It darkened even the strobing light generated from the Beast's undulating movement.

"Fine!" The rifleman dived into the cave and cried out as he slid and skidded towards an unknown fate.

"Nothing for it," Snipes said as he shoved Flayr down the rocky slide and turned to fire several more blasts into the mass of the creature surging upon him. It flinched and hesitated under his ballistic barrage, but it ultimately powered forth to crush him like a wave.

Snipes was struck by the feeling of the ground slipping out from beneath his feet, but steeled himself and dived onto the uneven ground of the cave. He let gravity carry him painfully away from the creature, which slammed into the cliff face with a colossal impact that shook the skeletal structure.

Snipes was sure that if there were any protrusions along his sliding path that could have been avoided, the Three Perversities had made sure that that was not the case.

He tumbled through concussive force, darkness, and nausea until finally he slid out of an exit and slammed onto hard, metallic ground on some kind of plateau.

Flayr and the rifleman were tentatively aiming their weapons at each other.

"No time for that, you moon rock morons!" Snipes forced himself to his feet and ran past them, the pink goo spilling out of the causeway behind them to rear up again. "Get up to those structures!"

Snipes bolted up a sinewy path towards what could only be described as hovels. They were grey, resin-like structures built into the skeletal plateau. Strange humanoid beings roamed about them, but Snipes was going to take his chances with them rather than the globular horror that was threatening to consume them.

Snipes turned halfway up the rise and fired his revolvers into the mass of the creature again. Multiple shots splattered into its surface, which rippled across its skin, and the monster wailed in response. Flayr was hobbling after him, left behind by the rifleman, who dashed in the other direction.

The poor rifleman spun and fired in a panic into the mass, and the beam from his prism rifle seared through a section of the creature that fell clean off with a wet sizzle. The creature took exception to this and changed directions, barrelling down solely on the lone rifleman, who shrieked in panic and sprinted for the edge of the plateau.

Flayr caught up to Snipes and hobbled past him into the strange village, as Snipes watched the strange hunt in morbid curiosity. The rifleman reached the edge of the plateau and leaped without looking, plummeting to whatever depths lay below. The blob crashed after him, spilling over the edge like a mud fall and falling out of sight.

"Poor bugger," Snipes sighed, and turned, only to freeze again. "Well ..."

The assembled villagers were standing around Flayr with crude weapons carved from resin chunks or from the very skeleton of the Beast they lived inside.

"Who are you?" one of the creatures said. They were thin and twig-like, looking of a similar substance of their grey, resin structures. Its voice was like what you imagine an ancient tree might sound like if it could talk. "Are you from the outer worlds?" From the strange headdress this creature wore, Snipes took him to be the leader of this village.

"In a manner of speaking," Flayr answered.

"Please," Snipes said, "we've been stranded here, and we need your help."

The elder looked at Snipes hard; its eye sockets were sunken black wells with two beady little points of light in their depths. "You are the first people we have seen to have wounded the Infyrra ..."

"The what?" Snipes asked.

"The cancer ... It has stripped our lands bare ever since the great famine. It is clear you are not from these parts, but you possess a warlike manner that we have not witnessed since our fighters left for the glands. We are defenceless and you need aid ... perhaps we can help each other?"

Snipes and Flayr eyed each other.

"I was worried you were going to suggest something like that," Snipes said.

CHAPTER 7

Votly

T umbling through the nether as sheer, uncontained waves of fractal light left only one thought in Votly's mind—*I'm alive?*

Votly knew it was possible, but to actually have done it was an experience in and of itself. High Prismatist Scrond would have blustered for the chance to study an uncontained living Wave-Form ignition ... but he was dead.

Sorrow for her mentor was quickly dulled by adrenaline, however, as the prospect of death reminded Votly of the danger she was just—and probably still was—in.

Votly pushed from the chunky soil that covered her and found herself in a jagged, alien mountain range with the shifting nebulous skies of the void high above her.

Her first instinct was to reach for her helmet and slam the visor down into place.

But she hesitated. It would have been too late already. She would already be dead if she were exposed to the open vacuum. And the stars, they twinkled with eddies and currents that swirled around an ephemeral barrier in such a strange way …

"Atmosphere," she breathed.

The air had a metallic tang to it and was heavy to breathe as if rife with moisture. As the mountain range shifted around her almost imperceptibly, a secretion of mist hissed into the air from cracks and joints and surfaces that appeared solid, but upon closer inspection she found that they were porous.

"Oh, this isn't good."

On the horizon, one of the mountains loomed, and then *kept looming*, growing higher and casting Votly in shadow as it rose over the edge of the world. She knew she was not on a typical world by now, of course; she just didn't want to accept it.

The mountain loomed even further before halting at its zenith. Then it lowered just as slowly back over the horizon. Votly realised she was holding her breath and gasped.

"Votly," her earpiece crackled.

Votly put her hand to her ear and turned away from the horrible sight of shifting continental masses. "This is Votly." Her airy voice came out in a quiet rasp. "I'm *on* the back of the Beast. Someone help me!"

"Votly, calm down. This is Sergeant Balt. I can see you up on the ridge … err … tailwards … from me."

Votly took a deep breath and searched the jagged landscape for the familiar sight of a prism marine. The rocks shifted and the blue-grey sleeve of Balt shot up from the rocks and waved her over.

With shaking legs, Votly traversed the rocky ridge until she hopped over the boulder and gasped. Balt—along with a squadron of beleaguered marines—was bivouacked in a little rocky ditch between jagged protrusions of the Beast's exoskeleton. A shadow passed overhead and Votly flinched, looking up to find one of the dozens of worlds orbiting above her and blotting out the starlit sky.

"Are you hurt?" Balt took her hand and guided her down into safety once the shadow had passed.

"And do you have any idea what in the blazing lights happened to us?" another marine groaned.

Votly was stricken by a wave of guilt. "Were any of you on the bridge?" she asked.

"Most of the marines here were down the corridor, fighting the mutineers and those ... things." Balt shuddered.

"They called themselves Slithmet." Votly's lip quivered. She could still feel the press of its talons against her skin, and she absentmindedly touched her cut face. "They took over the bridge and forced me to trigger the Wave-Form sequence before the engines had properly cooled."

The marines stopped fidgeting and stared at her. They were no scientists, but even the least educated Prismath knew what that would entail.

"How in shards are we still alive?" one of the marines cried.

Votly shrugged. "Luck?" She thought briefly of Tara. "I tried to cancel the sequence when there was a distraction, but I was too late ... I'm sorry."

"So you did this to us?" A marine stumbled to his feet and drew his energy knife.

Balt rose to stop him but halted. The marine triggered the current to pass through the knife, and it vibrated violently, and then was pulled from his hand to stick to the ground.

"This creature produces an electromagnetic field," Votly squeaked. "Your knife essentially becomes a super magnet when it's activated. I would suggest if you wanted to kill me you use it as a standard blade."

"No one is going to kill you," Balt said pointedly. "Right lads?" He gazed at the marines. "And … ladettes?"

"Newsflash, Balt," one of the marines said. She had rose-coloured skin and copper hair. She stalked over to Balt and Votly as the first marine deactivated and sheathed his knife. Her face was grazed and dried blue blood clung to her lips. "This techie could have jettisoned us all across the sun well with her little stunt."

"One of our primary tenets is to never let our ship fall into enemy hands." Votly looked down bashfully. "It's our people's greatest resource … I … I thought it was better to activate it before they had a chance to figure out it needed to cool! And then when I had the opportunity, I tried to stop it."

"You thought you were killing us?" Balt said solemnly.

Votly nodded without speaking.

The marines groaned and swore. "Then let's be rid of her," one said. "We've got other problems. I saw a few of our traitorous buddies milling around tailwards; this fight isn't over."

"You want to kill a member of the command crew, yet you have the gall to call the riflemen traitors?" Balt's voice could have cut through lead. The marine quieted. "We were all going to die in that mutiny; those creatures would have done who knows what to us. When everyone was beaten Votly made the hardest choice there was to make. She will lead us out of this mess."

Votly nearly squeaked, "Me?"

"You *are* the highest-ranking officer present," Balt said.

"B-but, but I'm just a techie. I was a Prismatist in training, that's it!"

"Newsflash, techie ..." the woman marine started.

"Stop saying newsflash," Balt interjected. But the marine continued on unperturbed.

"... But you led us all into this mess, so you're the one who has to take responsibility and lead us out!"

Votly glanced around the beleaguered marines with a harried, increasingly frantic fluttering of eyelids and an incessant sweat dripping down her brow. Her eyes froze on Balt, who pushed up his goggles and gave her a reassuring look. One that told her he was there to back her up.

"All right," she breathed through her teeth, "all right, just ... let me think." She plonked herself onto the granular surface and brought up her wrist-mounted light lab, or light gauntlet as Tara had called it. She flicked lenses and light toggles into position, and a miniature hologram splayed into display before the squadron of marines.

"This is our approximate location on the back of the Beast, extrapolated from our relative position at the time of boarding." A little image of the *Motebeam* filtered into view and hovered before the representation of the Beast in a scattering of light beams. "These are all predicted paths for everyone who was on board. The *Dustmote* is ... sorry, the *Motebeam* is ..." She blushed, not meaning to use her nickname for the ship in front of everyone else. She toggled more switches, and the image of the *Motebeam* flung itself straight into the Beast's maw "… somewhere in the innards. We smashed into its upper mouth and split its skull, poor thing."

"They were trying to kill the Beast?" Balt asked.

"I don't think so. I think they wanted inside its brain," Votly answered.

"So we're trapped here?" A marine who was on watch looked back from his perch on a spine.

"No, not necessarily," Votly said. "It's possible that the *Motebeam* survived, and that not all crew were scattered. It is highly likely that only people on the front end of the vessel would have been scattered away from the ship."

"So, mostly every combatant?" Balt scratched the stubble on his chin and slumped against the ditch.

"Yes, but it means that the tech crews could be repairing any damage to our vessel even as we speak. And I know the marines still had control over the engine room. So that's something. What we have to do is regroup, contact the captain somehow, and get to the *Motebeam* before the riflemen or their Slithmet friends do."

"I was fighting in the corridors before we were blasted across space," the woman who had stalked over to her said. "We were heavily outnumbered to begin with against the riflemen, and we took heavy losses in the initial betrayal. We're going to have the fight of our lives."

"That's why we need to regroup," Votly said. "I think Tara said something about these creatures being in league with the Rel, and they convinced the riflemen otherwise … and then they executed Bromean once he was of no use to them." She suppressed a sob, shook her head, and pointed at her Light

Gauntlet again. "There." Her hologram expanded to include the orbiting worlds and more light beams representing the potential path of the scattered crew. "The best thing I can see to do is to get to that spine peak," she pointed to the mountain that was dipping below the horizon, "and broadcast a distress signal that should reach all parties on all of the worlds."

"Including the traitors," the marine on watch said.

"And the locals," Balt said. "They might not be friendly."

"It's a risk, but we need to regroup. We only have a few days before this Beast reaches our world. If Mallel is alive, he won't forsake us," Votly said. *I need him to be alive, and Tara.*

The marines were silent; Votly knew if they didn't trust her leadership, they at least trusted Captain Mallel.

"Then we're agreed." Balt slapped his knee and pushed himself up, shouldering his prism rifle. "Up you get, marines; we've got a family dispute to resolve!"

The squadron grumbled as they picked themselves up and readied to make way. The woman with rose-coloured skin shuffled over to Votly. "Don't get us killed," she said.

Votly gulped. "I'll do my best."

"I'm Curla, by the way, Corporal Curla."

"Votly," Votly squeaked.

"I know." She shoved past Votly. "Now stay on my six and take this." She turned back and handed Votly a prism pistol. "There are riflemen out there, and those creatures."

Votly shook her head. "I have my own."

"Where?" Curla looked her up and down.

Votly absentmindedly reached for her hip holster, to find it was not there. She looked down in bewilderment; the straps had been cut clean through when the Slithmet had taken her hostage.

"Exactly," Curla grunted, shoving the pistol into Votly's hands. "Now let's go."

Votly gripped the weapon in cold, feeble fingers. Her peach complexion was much brighter now that her dark blue blood had retreated from her skin. She took a deep breath, and pushed on to stay behind Curla and Balt as they exited their little hidey hole on the spine of the cosmic Beast they were marooned on.

"Where's this peak we're going to?" Balt asked, scanning the undulating horizon.

"Look tailwards and wait a minute ... there." Votly pointed to the mountain that loomed up from the starlit sky. It was a rising spire of craggy, metallic, rock-like spine plate.

"Roger that," Balt breathed in awe. "We move tailwards. Private, take point."

A marine nodded and spirited forward into the alien rockscape, darting from cover to cover as the party traversed the ridges behind him.

A beam of red light lanced out from the ridge across from them. The private cried out, "Shards!" and dived for cover.

Curla raised her rifle in one quick reflex and fired back on the place the shot had originated from.

"You missed me, you wench!" a horridly familiar voice cried out from the ridges.

"Go!" Curla said in a harsh whisper.

Votly kept her head down and sped past her as sporadic potshots from marines and riflemen lit up the grey landscape. Every beam of prism-focused energy illuminated the magnetic eddies of metallic dust with brilliant, radiant auroras. The aftereffects of each shot danced with kaleidoscopic brilliance.

"Anyone wounded?" Balt grabbed a smoke bomb—crafted and gifted to him by Tara—and tossed it over the rock he used for cover.

"Negative, Sergeant," Curla answered. "Just a bit annoyed."

"I bet." Balt chuckled. There was a blast from the bomb, and a cloud of smoke rose into the air in strange swirling patterns as the smoke particles interacted with the flowing magnetic dust in the air. "Move!" Balt barked.

The marines took their opportunity to dart over the next ridge and out of sight of the harassing party before the smoke cleared.

"Orders, Votly?" Balt breathed hard.

Votly still meekly gripped her pistol in both hands. "W-we need to contact Captain Mallel. We push on."

Under the constant fire from former comrades in arms, the marines shuffled down the spine of the Beast in a haphazard fashion.

CHAPTER 8

Tara Star

The walk from the outskirts of this little trailing world was rather pleasant compared to Tara's initial half-suffocated stumbling. The air was relatively fresh—somehow—despite the horrid odours that spewed from the random geysers of gas about the place. And her companion, while slow, seemed to amble on with graciousness and appreciation for her assistance.

"You see, those kids are brought up thinking all outsiders are the enemy. Granted, many outsiders were enemies in the years that preceded this little incident," Hoztic said.

"So you're not from around here either?" Tara pulled off her coat and started disassembling the void suit she wore, leaving it in pieces behind her as they marched.

She felt lighter and more nimble with each successive removal of heavy equipment.

"Not quite. I am from ..." He paused. "Well, nowhere really. Our world was tacked onto the Great One's tail during the galactic arm migration."

"I only understand some of those words." Tara furrowed her brow. "Why did you hesitate?"

Hoztic frowned. "There was a war, and my world disintegrated."

"Oh ..." Tara said, and the tingling flared. "Just like the Slithmet's?"

Hoztic did not answer immediately. "Most of the worlds that orbit this thing began in another part of the cosmos ... You think I am like that thing you found back there?" He gestured to his diminutive body.

Tara trundled on, the Luck Symbioid flaring violently now. "I don't know what anything around here is. But you aren't like the vicious thing that attacked my friends. I am sorry for the loss of your world." Hoztic did not answer, so Tara spoke to break the silence. "Is that the town?"

A cluster of stone buildings rose on the horizon, which was periodically overshadowed by the propelling tail of the titanic Beast that the little world orbited around. Tara had to keep reminding herself that the colossal sight was normal here, that their world wasn't going to collide into the creature, and that the Beast would not on a whim decide to devour them in one bite.

Hoztic told her the Beast fed on nebula clouds, taking in minerals and water. And that much of the water on this world was farmed from the sweating process that kept the Beast from overheating. Tara had to stop herself from gagging as she watched clouds and mists siphon from the joints in the creature as it moved.

"Whatever you need to do to survive," Tara had responded.

Now the town was coming into sight, and Tara had to suppress another exclamation, not of anger or fear, but of bewilderment. "You've got to be joking ..."

"What? What is it?" Hoztic asked, concerned.

A familiar tune jaunted along the air, coming from somewhere within the town ... a jaunty, piano jig tune.

"A Jaunt Saloon?"

"Yes?" Hoztic said.

"There's a gear-jammed Jaunt Saloon on this tiny little rock hurtling around a titanic space monster on the edge of the sun well?" Tara could not believe her ears. Of all the impossibilities over the last day, this was too much.

Hoztic cocked his serpentine head at her. "Tara, there is a Jaunt Saloon in every town, wherever ..."

"... Wherever the wilderness of the underworld meets civilisation," Tara interrupted Hoztic, "a Jaunt Saloon will be there to fill the information demand." Tara had heard the phrase during her assassin training every time they covered target reconnaissance. "I just thought that was secluded to my own world ... my own continent even."

"What's a continent?" Hoztic peered up at her.

Tara looked at Hoztic a moment, and then took his stubby little taloned hand in hers. "Come on, we need information, and now there's a place to get it!"

"Wait!" Hoztic cried. "The townspeople here might not be very receptive to me. I need you to get me to the Jaunt Saloon anyway so I can find more of my people, but I need a safe way to get there ..." He eyed her up and down.

Tara frowned. "How flexible are you?"

"I can fit into very tight places," Hoztic responded.

Tara sighed and held her coat open. "Very well, curl around my body under my jacket, and I'll button it up."

Hoztic eyed her again, up and down for a moment, and then sidled up to Tara with tentative steps. He took a breath and slithered around her body under her coat and nestled his head against her side where he could peek out from one of her buttonholes.

He was quite light, Tara realised, and when he pressed flat against her, it was as good a hiding spot as there could be. "Right," Tara said, fastening her jacket closed. "Let's get you to your people, and let's get me to mine!"

"After you," Hoztic sniggered.

Tara marched into the town, looking a little bulkier than she had previously. Hoztic might have been a slight, wormlike creature, but with him nestled beneath her coat, she now had an asymmetrical belly.

The town itself was what you would get if you took a countryside slum but constructed it out of meteorite carvings. That was the best way Tara could rationalise what she saw in her mind. Instead of shanty lean-tos, the market stalls she found on the cramped, winding streets were constructed of corrugated iron and propped open with strange signs that danced with neon lights.

And that was just the buildings. The people of this world who crowded into the tight streets and markets were as varied as they could be, and Tara squealed in delight.

It was a hustle and bustle of many strange species. Some were big and bulbous like the hoodlums Tara had fought earlier, and others were like twisted rock, or slimy, or scaly.

All the different kinds of people possessed an air of humanoid-ish-ness, in the sense that they had a body and limbs and a face of some sort.

Tara quickly stopped squealing and forced herself to focus. She remarkably felt quite at ease. When all things were considered, this was just another town like all the others she had been to as an outsider.

There were the family-run food stalls, packed to the brim with steaming goodness; there were street urchins on the corner, pretending to beg as they picked at pockets; there were the couples who swayed through the chaos arm in arm ... just an ordinary town.

Tara let the familiarity wash over her—it was the only way she could deal with the accompanying strangeness.

Here also there would be law and order, underbellies of crime, and the inevitable entangling of the two, with their own customs and rules. The prospect of learning the new cultures and territories and the like would overwhelm a newer adventurer, but all Tara felt was bliss. There would be no time to immerse herself in this place, however. She had to regroup with the crew of the *Motebeam*, with Snipes, Votly ... and Mallel.

She hoped Mallel was all right.

The majority of the throng stopped to gawk at her as she passed through, winding around the labyrinthine streets as she followed the sound of the jaunty piano jig tune. But mostly they went about their business. She was an outsider, yes, but this place seemed used to strange people.

"Would any of these people attack me?" Tara whispered into her coat. "Like those kids attacked you?"

"You aren't more likely to be attacked here than any other backwater town you've been to," Hoztic's muffled voice replied.

"Then why did they attack you?" Tara whispered again.

"My people were once at war with the majority of theirs … You might do well to abandon me here if I am discovered."

The tingling flared so brightly, Tara winced.

"Not while I need a guide through these strange new lands," Tara hissed against the tingling pain. "You can help me avoid a brawl or two at the Jaunt Saloon, or, controversially, you can help me start one if I need." She laughed.

"Extra! Extra! Read all about it!" They passed a street urchin with webbed green feet waving an embossed stone slate. "The price of trade route protection has dropped as all Slithmet raiding parties head towards the Great One's skull! It was smashed open by a celestial event, and the remaining Custanguin have rallied by the breach, leaving the rest of the body defenceless against disease. Expect sweat supplies to drop as we swim further away from nebulas. Gland wars have intensified, so unless you travel with a licensed war band, rethink your travel plans to the body and stick to the orbiting worlds."

"So the Rel *do* want into the skull," Tara hissed as they bustled past the newsboy.

"Rel …" Hoztic cocked his head within the jacket, "… I have heard stories of these Rel. You think the Slithmet are in league with them?"

"I know they are." Tara tapped her head. "I have this thing called a symbioid in my body that can detect and resist the Rel. These Slithmet fiends are in league with them, all right."

Hoztic rolled the word around his snout. "Symbioid ... is it ... could it be useful in stopping the Slithmet?"

"I hope so ... Cogrust!" Tara stopped and hit her head.

"Are you all right?" Hoztic peered up at her through her coat; his dull red eyes swam with tendrils of ...

NO! Tara gritted her teeth as she yelled at the Luck Symbioid in her mind. "I am fine," Tara hissed. "Let's just get to the saloon. It sounds close now."

They rounded a bend and found their destination; the Jaunt Saloon looked much like the ones she had encountered back on Stemcog—her world. It was a squat, two-storied building constructed of wooden slats that bulged at the seams with its haphazard construction.

All manner of alien miscreant and thug lounged about the balconies on the outside, enjoying watching another fistfight break out or nursing their heads after finishing their own one. The raucous, seedy atmosphere bled out of the place and into the surrounding streets.

"Excellent." Tara beamed. "Shall we?" She pushed through the slat door, and as she entered, the player piano did something it had never done at any Jaunt Saloon she had visited before—it stopped. All eyes turned towards her, whether they were stalks or strange sunken depressions in a skull-like face.

Her heart fluttered in her chest, anxiety momentarily overriding her training before it subsided. They weren't looking at her ... They were looking at Hoztic, whose head had slipped out of the front of her coat.

"These people really don't like you," Tara murmured under her breath as she stepped into the bar, the floorboards creaking in the silence.

"Like I said, my kind was once at war with many of theirs," Hoztic croaked as he slunk back into her coat. "I thought some of my stronger companions would be here by now. These people would mob me without protection."

"I'll protect you," Tara whispered, sauntering through the gauntlet of glares while nodding at the ruffians.

She eyed down at Hoztic; he was this small, gangly thing. How could his kind ever be a threat? How much stronger could his companions be? There must be more to this story, but there was a time to ask such questions. And if this was the time, it had just ended when a saloon full of alien bounty hunters eyed her with sinister intent. Tara slowly made her way past the bar—nodding at the bulbous, overflowing mass that she assumed was the barman as he pumped thick sludge into tankards—and made her way to the notice board.

"You after information, stranger?" A creature that resembled a kaleidoscope of scales slithered up to her from the shadows. "Turning in a bounty perhaps?" Its eyes flittered down her coat to Hoztic.

"I'm just browsing," Tara said. "This ... fellow ... owes me a life debt."

"Ah," the barman blustered. "So this cur is off-limits to all of you drunken fools!" It slammed a gelatinous mass of an arm over the bar. "Get that jaunty tune playing!"

The piano—without visible intervention—started playing again, and the bar returned to its usual raucous din.

"Just be careful there, stranger," the scaly creature said, slinking back into the shadows. "His kind ..."

"Yeah, yeah," Tara waved him off, "I'll watch my back. Any other strangers come through here recently? People looking like me ... somewhat like me?"

"Can't say that I know much about strangers … other than a pretty light show that scattered through the orbits a couple of hours ago."

"Any of those lights land nearby?" Tara asked.

The scaled head cocked at her, dim neon lighting reflecting out of one of its sly eyes.

Tara sighed and produced a cube, a green one, and tossed it to the scaly creature.

"What's this?" it said, turning the cube over in taloned hands.

"A fair amount of currency in the direction this big beastie is heading," Tara said.

"Hmm, here we use chits, stranger."

"Do you barter?"

The scaled thing hissed, "What do you have to offer?"

Tara produced a bundle of her throwing knives. "Perfectly balanced," she said, "and easy to conceal."

The creature reached out and took them, and after a moment, it tossed the green cube back to her. "There was one that landed not too far off."

"That was me."

"Ah … Another landed in the gravity shallows, not too far away. Bad place that is, lots of miscreants. I've heard there's been a kafuffle."

"Can you point me in the direction of the shallows?"

Hoztic cleared his throat. "It's near a way station between some of the orbiting worlds. I can show you."

The scaled thing grimaced. "Just be careful, stranger. His kind …"

"Yeah, yeah, yeah." Tara turned from the colourful, scaly creature and made to leave the saloon.

Her ears twitched. From beyond the swinging doors, there was a skittering, chitinous sound. It was not unlike the sound the Slithmet made when they boarded the *Motebeam*.

"Cogrust!" Tara dashed into one of the unoccupied shadowy booths as a silhouette of a Slithmet loomed over the swinging slat doors and burst in.

The player piano went silent again, replaced by the flapping, swinging doors behind the Slithmet. All eyes turned towards the monster with the sound of unsheathing blades, guns being cocked, and strange energy weapons being primed.

"Peace," the Slithmet hissed, slinking into the den of debauchery. "I am here to issue a bounty." It slithered around the potential enemies and up to the notice board, producing a sheet of paper which it pinned in place. "There are a number of strangers around these parts; one of their leaders currently defends himself in the gravity shallows. My kind would pay dearly for him to be delivered to us ... alive."

"There are those who would pay dearly for your exosuit, Slithmet," one of the patrons said, a stone-skinned creature with bulky shoulders. "With you in it mangled and dead."

"Exosuit," Tara breathed. "Those things are piloted machines?"

Hoztic tensed under her coat. "You did not notice their mechanical nature when they boarded your *Dustmote*?"

Her tingling flared. *Dustmote* ... Only Votly called it the *Dustmote*, and she uttered that name on the bridge when the Slithmet took her hostage ... *Okay*, she thought, addressing the tingling that was screaming for her attention. *I get it ... I know ...*

"Hush," she said aloud. "Do not draw attention."

The Slithmet coiled and rounded on the patron, who flinched back. "Then come and claim it, stoneling." It splayed its talons with a spark. "We'll see who mangles who."

"One of your dweeb friends was in here just a moment ago." The colourful, scaly creature stepped into the light again, his eyes glinting, "He was very shy; it seems you lot only have a spine when you're in your exosuits."

The Slithmet rounded on the scaly creature, slowly. "Where is my compatriot?"

Okay, Tara thought as her heart hammered in her chest. She thought again, directly responding to the flaring Luck Symbioid. *I get it. The Slithmet I fought on the* Motebeam *and the wiry creature wrapped around my body right now are the same person. Its suit was destroyed beyond use, and I just saved and aided a monster that wants me and my kind dead ...* The Luck Symbioid flared in a way that could only be described as a sigh of relief. *I should have trusted you ...* she thought again ... *I'm sorry.*

Beneath her coat, she felt Hoztic's dull talons flex— at least he wasn't that much of a threat at the moment. Hopefully he hadn't realised that *she* had realised what he was ... She was going to have to think of a way to get out of this predicament, safely.

"What's the bounty?" A voice cut through the growing hubbub of people gearing up to fight.

"Three thousand chits," the Slithmet hissed, turning away from the scaly creature. "Alive."

One of the patrons whistled while the rest settled down, sheathing their weapons.

The owner of the new voice stalked out from the dank corner of the saloon, each step clinking against the sagging floorboards as mercenaries parted for her. Tara sensed danger, and her Luck Symbioid flared in agreement. This huntress was tall, sleek, and more humanoid than many of the other beings that inhabited this rock. She wore a calf-length coat with slits up to her hips, and her gait was punctuated by clinking spurs that jutted out from her stilettos. Hanging from her hip was a coil of cord with a wicked-looking barb strapped to the end—a rope dart—and she wore a tricorne hat, like the sailors on Stemcog would wear. It was black with gold trimmings.

Her face was vaguely humanlike, with elongated features protruding out from the rim of her hat.

"For three thousand chits, I might just fight every cutthroat in this dive to protect you, just so that you can pay me afterwards." She tilted her head and smiled, a gesture that would have turned heads in another context ... Tara only felt her skin crawl.

The Slithmet bared its fangs. "He's in the gravity shallows giving what is left of my war band a bit of trouble. You might want to keep some of these cutthroats around for backup. We're trying to round them up before they can regroup ... They're dangerous once they get together."

Could they be talking about Mallel? Tara thought. Her Luck Symbioid tingled, a response that even she could not force herself to ignore. *Mallel ... now our enemy has raised a bounty against him, and he is already under siege. I'll have to move quickly.*

"Dibs!" The stone-skinned mercenary that initially threatened the Slithmet stood and stormed out the doors, only for a whip crack to follow in his wake.

The rope dart around the woman's hip had unfurled with a deft motion and snapped out. The dart slammed into the mercenary's skull before she yanked it back and pulled the stoneling's lifeless corpse to crumble onto the ground.

"Ladies first." She chuckled, striding over the corpse. "You make those chits out to me, Cronetta Lesh." She pushed through the slat doors, and they swung back once, twice, three times before half the saloon picked themselves up and charged after her.

The bounty of a lifetime had been issued, Tara realised, and Mallel didn't have much time.

"Now where is that 'dweeb' friend of mine?" The Slithmet waited in the saloon as it emptied of over half of the bounty hunters. Those that stayed eyed the Slithmet warily with their hands on their weapons. Its red eyes scanned them and the empty booths, homing in on hers.

It knows I'm here ... Tara realised. *No, the Rel Scion within it knows there's a Rel Scion here with Hoztic under my cogrusted coat!*

"Are we going to go help your friend?" Hoztic wheezed.

"That depends, friend ..." Tara glanced at the player piano—the Luck Symbioid flared gently—it knew she was listening to it now ... for the moment.

The barman squelched more sludge into another tankard. "You going to be buying a drink soon?" he asked the Slithmet. "Because your tail is scratching my floor, and I'll need compensation."

The Slithmet turned and hissed at the barman, "Insolent fool, I would see your whole establishment crumble just so that I don't have to hear that monstrosity again!" It pointed a wicked talon at the player piano.

"Hey!" one of the remaining patrons barked. "*No one* messes with the player piano!"

"Silence, worm!" The Slithmet rounded on the new voice. "The only one here who was capable of defeating me is now on my payroll. You're nothing!"

Hoztic writhed under Tara's coat; he was gearing to make a move. "You better think of something soon, dear Tara. If my compatriot doesn't sense me, I will simply call out to him. And you won't kill a defenceless old man like me."

So, Tara realised with a humourless smile. *The jig is up.*

"Like you killed poor Bromean?" she asked.

"Exactly! Know it was for a good cause; now the skull of the Great One is open to us. The Rel partially directed the Great One to your sun well, but with us in control of the brain stem, we can *ensure* it feeds on your worlds, and then we can use it to control the fate of all for the betterment of my people. All we have to do is get to it before you do. We may be scattered after that blasted ship crashed ... but so are you."

So the Beast isn't necessarily a threat unless we can get to the skull. "Then," Tara spoke slowly, preparing herself for the coming flight, "a race. First one to the skull gets to save their own world ... I guess."

"You'll never win," Hoztic said. "And even if you do, do you think your Captain Mallel will redirect the Great One like you know you want. Or will he try to kill it, and damn everyone who lives on these worlds? Yes, Tara, the Rel Scion within me knows of your conflicts."

Tara hesitated.

"While you flounder with your moral dilemmas …" Hoztic continued, "I'll have a new exosuit as soon as I've wriggled out of your grasp, and with it I will skin your writhing form." He dug into Tara's side with his talons.

"Cogrust!" The other Slithmet rounded on the noise, but Tara reacted quickly.

She grabbed Hoztic by the neck and wrenched him from her coat—pulling him from her like ripping off a belt—and launched him at the player piano. With a yelp he crashed through it, and the piano disintegrated with a horrid death knell note.

"Hey …" the barman started, but Tara was taking advantage of the situation already.

"That Slithmet crony broke the player piano! Get him!" She then dashed out of the swinging doors.

The Slithmet reared to go after her, but was mobbed by the remaining patrons in a close-quarters brawl before it could react.

Tara hit the metallic soil running and tore after the dust cloud left by the band of ravenous bounty hunters. Sounds of intense conflict were erupting from the saloon in her wake.

"Okay," she said aloud, "I should start listening to you more!" The tingling flared down her spine. "But don't think this means I like you! Now we've got to get to Mallel before that Cronetta Lesh does."

The tingling flared again.

"Don't be a lump of wet coal! Just get me to Mallel before he dies!"

With that, she quickened her pace, tearing after the band of mercenaries ahead of her.

CHAPTER 9

Snipes

nipes pressed a damp cloth into Flayr's partially cauterised shoulder wound. She gasped and flinched back, but Snipes kept a firm grasp on her.

"It'll be over soon," he said gently.

"Doesn't feel like it," Flayr huffed through pursed lips.

Snipes smiled at her. "Soon," he promised. "So, this infected cell ..." Snipes then said over his shoulder.

"Infyrra," the chieftain corrected, and he rattled his staff in a warding motion. "We have faced its kind before. Our people live off the Great One's innards, tending to its needs much like its own Custanguin do."

"Right ..." Snipes eyed Flayr and whispered, "*Custanguin?*"

She shrugged. A wisp of matted bronze fell across her scalp and stuck there. She was burning up; that wasn't good.

"They're the immune cells. They help us in our sacred duties," the chieftain continued, "but if not respected, they can turn violent. A decade ago, this Infyrra emerged from the depths and started stripping them of their flesh, growing stronger and more insatiable. Eventually it turned on us and started gnawing on the tissue and bone of our great benefactor. We have few Custanguin left to protect our benefactor, and its health is failing. And to make matters worse, the Custanguin that were here in the bowels have moved either towards the Great One's skull or towards its tail. We believe they will not be back in time to stop this monstrosity."

Snipes turned to look the chieftain straight in his beady little eyes. "The Great One ... you mean the Beast we are inside of?"

"Yes, of course." The chieftain cocked his gangly head. "Are you not aware of what gives us life?"

"I don't know if you realise this ... sir, but we aren't from around these parts."

"So I've gathered." He chuckled, jostling his rattling staff with the motion. "And you've come here because?" He leaned in and smiled politely.

"We told you we're stranded," Flayr sighed. "Our ship scattered itself across the void for all we know."

"Oh, oh oh oh oh!" One of the tribe members—a little kid—was hopping up and down with his hand in the air. "I saw that! I saw that! It slammed into the Infyrra! I saw that!"

"Quiet, boy." One of the women hushed the child.

Snipes stood up. "No, shut up." He waved the mother away and pointed sternly at the kid. "You saw a giant rainbow slam into that globular menace, and you're only now just speaking up about it?"

The kid looked down at his feet, bashfully. "The Infyrra was coming out of the tummy. It was about to get me when the light hit it, and it ran back into the bowels for a while before coming back out. That's when we saw you running through the marrow canals."

Snipes took a moment to suppress a shudder at "marrow canals" and cleared his throat. "So our ship is in the bowels ..."

"And it is guarded by the Infyrra." The chieftain sighed, looked away, then eyed Snipes coyly. "It seems you must venture into the depths and kill it."

"Cogrust," Snipes whispered. "You'll need to look after my friend here while I head down to locate it."

"We will keep her safe, mark my words." The chieftain picked up one of his necklaces and rattled it. Snipes took that—he hoped—as a binding oath.

The crowds cleared out of the little hovel they were crammed into, and Snipes turned back to Flayr. "I'll need your prism rifle; the Infyrra got my gun."

"While I, what?" Flayr pushed up from her cot with a frown. "Stay here like some damsel in distress?"

"Hey," Snipes caressed the strand of matted hair from her brow, "you aren't a damsel in distress to me. You're more like ... like ..."

"Yes?" She gazed up into his eyes with longing.

"Right now you're more like a client."

Flayr slumped back, crossing her arms. "Oh."

"Now you stay safe." Snipes picked up her prism rifle. "These people will look after you. I'll get to the *Motebeam* and see if anyone onboard it is still alive. Hopefully the right members of the crew survived, and I'll come back and get you." He smiled and stalked out of the hovel.

Flayr sat there in the silence for a moment, brow furrowed, before Snipes stalked back in, leaned down, and kissed her on the forehead. "Goodbye."

She kissed him back and then said, "Snipes, take this." She pulled out the comms device from her ear. "If you get close to the *Motebeam*, you might be able to communicate with anyone still inside."

Snipes took it and wedged it in his ear uncertainly; he looked down at her, nodded, and left a second time.

CHAPTER 10

Votly

It was a hard slog pressing down the spine of the cosmic Beast under the constant strafing of prism beam fire. But the marines Votly was running with were the best of the best. They were elite soldiers selected from the ranks of Prismath's fighters for their aptitude, which was honed with intense training.

Their enemy the riflemen, while hardy and more numerous, were lesser trained and lesser equipped.

With precise shots that tore through the magnetosphere with fractal auroras of multicoloured light, the riflemen were kept at bay enough for the marines—and Votly—to duck from cover to cover.

There was an emerging issue, however, as the mad-dash fighting continued up the spine of the Beast, uphill now as its body undulated throughout the cosmos.

There were several problems with this situation, Votly realised. The first was that while the marines and the riflemen were both scattered throughout the area, the rolling battle was attracting more of the dispersed enemy to converge on the marines' location. Balt and Curla called the shots on the front two flanks as fresh foes emerged, trading a barrage of magnetically induced kaleidoscopic fire from multiple angles. Surely there were a few marines in those scattered outskirts who were trying to link up with the fleeing group, but as cut off as they were, they may as well have been leagues away.

The second problem was that this rolling battle meant they could not progress at as quick a pace as Votly would like. Every time she glanced at her Light Gauntlet, she could feel the seconds slipping away as the Beast drew closer to their world.

If they could not find a way to stop it in time, all was lost; and any attempt to yell this out to the riflemen was met with jeers and beam fire.

The third problem was about to present itself.

The undulation of the Beast's swim shifted, and the rising spire ahead of them that marked a segment of its spine crested, reaching the zenith of its movement. The marines found themselves on the precipice of the peak, vastly higher than the assaulting riflemen.

"We've got the high ground!" Balt roared and took position on a stony surface, firing over the heads of the marines as the group hurried past him.

"Not for long, though," Votly hissed. "The creature is still moving. In five minutes our high ground will snap below our pursuers, and we'll be at the bottom of a ravine. Unless we can kill all of the enemy in the next five minutes, we may as well shatter to shards right now!"

Curla swore, "Shards," as she peeked over cover to see the kaleidoscopic miasma of enemy fire ricocheting off the magnetic slope. "My gut's dropping; the Beast is already lowering us down." She shot sporadically down the slope, which was very quickly starting to flatten out.

"There's no way we can take them out. The cover is too great; we'll be pinned down," another marine cried.

"Then this is our last stand!" Balt snapped, drawing his prism pistol. "We have a chance if we charge on the flat and engage them in close quarters. At least man to man they won't be able to bring all of their rifles to bear against us."

Votly was frantically swiping through the holographic display on her Light Gauntlet, searching for anything in the surrounding landscape to aid them. "No Balt, that's suicide."

He smiled grimly at her. "Look, we did our best, but ultimately the deck was stacked against us."

"No!" Votly kept swiping. "If we hold to the flat, there might be something on the other side of the shrinking peak. The readings are odd."

"Hate to break it to you, techie," Curla said, "but odd readings aren't going to help us."

"Neither is suicidally charging into overwhelming odds!" Votly snapped. "You said I was in charge; my orders are to hold!"

Balt hesitated as he drew his energy cutlass. "Shards!" He rammed the blade back into its sheath. "All right, marines, you heard the lady. As soon as the peak drops, we leg it!"

"Any more smoke bombs from that assassin?" Curla asked.

Balt shook his head. "I'll stay here, try and pick off as many as I can."

"No." Votly bit down on her resolve—she wasn't sure what qualities she possessed that made her officer worthy, or worthy enough to be selected by Scrond himself for Prismatist training, but she knew that Mallel would not leave a marine behind so that he could escape.

"What?" Curla spun on Votly, ducking as a stray prism beam tore through the magnetic air in a dazzling display of refraction. "What else is there to do? The fire here is too concentrated."

"Concentrated ..." Votly breathed, her eyes lighting up.

She shoved past Curla and flipped up a large lens on her Light Gauntlet. She held it over the ridge as if it was a wrist-mounted weapon, and waited.

The next shot came out of the jagged landscape, and with a yelp of adrenaline, Votly manoeuvred her wrist to catch the brunt of the blow. The fractalling beam struck the large magnifying lens with a jolt that nearly tore her shoulder out of its socket. The energy concentrated, directing into the actuators and prisms that lined the working mechanisms of the gauntlet. The light intensified to the point the marines around her had to shield their eyes, but Votly squinted through the glare. Her arm shook violently with the ricocheting energy bouncing back and forth between the prisms and lenses in her device, magnifying, concentrating, and humming with power.

With a cry from Votly, the concentrated beam of energy then shot back out towards the magnifying lens on the wrist mount. Votly's hair ruffled with a wash of heat as wavelengths of every colour of light exploded from the lens. The blast shot into the magnetosphere in a blinding flare of technicoloured light.

The flare scattered in the magnetic currents, sparking as bright as a cluster of suns. The light from each spark pierced deep into the magnetosphere and shot waves of pulsing radiance back across the now rising slopes that their enemy fired from.

What Votly had just done was capture a beam of energy from a prism rifle and used Wave-Form to partially materialise it into matter. It shot out of her Light Gauntlet in an ejection of coronal-like plasma that caused the riflemen to cry out in alarm and dive for cover. And luckily they did, as the waves of brimming energy scalded the metallic rock faces they used to hide.

The light died after breaking upon the magnetic stone like a wave would break upon the shore, and the shocking silence that followed it was punctuated by cursing riflemen.

Votly turned to her ragtag group of bewildered marines.

"Why didn't you do that from the start?" Curla asked.

Votly tore the smouldering lens from her gauntlet and threw it away with a yelp as it singed her fingers. "Because it was a last resort. Now move it, marines, up the rise!" She pulled a smaller lens from her belt and inserted it into the gauntlet as she gave the order.

The marines upped and turned now that the riflemen were blinded. Votly wasn't sure if they were permanently blinded, or concussed, or hurt, or if they were just stunned senseless by whatever had happened, but she knew she didn't want to wait around to find out. She led the retreat down the other side of the peak as the Beast swayed through the cosmos. The slope they dashed down became a slope that they had to dash *up*.

Only they had to halt again, as their way was blocked by another conflict ahead of them.

Shrapnel and limbs flew this way and that in a maelstrom of close-quarter blows. There were two forces: one consisted of strange, metallic exoskeleton creatures, and the other was a band of pudgy, calloused, muscle-bound behemoths. They were engaged in a brutal match of slicing and bludgeoning.

It seemed that the more fleshy force was having the worse go of it. Their leader—judging from the wire crown it sported—was struggling with no less than four of the exoskeleton creatures as they were caught in a grapple. His skin was being torn and sliced as he walloped about them with an enormous metal club.

Neither side seemed to have the advantage in a one-on-one fight. It was just that the muscle-bound brutes were at the moment outmanoeuvred. Perhaps they were caught off guard by the swimming motion of the Beast much like the marines were a moment ago. Hard edges collided with callused mass, and the churning battle now raged down the temporary ravine towards Votly and her band.

"Ah … Orders?" Curla looked at Votly.

Votly drew her borrowed prism pistol. "They aren't concerned with us. Power through them and hope the melee covers us from the riflemen!"

As the marines drew closer to the battle, they found themselves reaching the top of the next peak as it reached its zenith. The top where these strange people fought each other was within prism rifle range of the peak behind them, where the riflemen were now recovering from Votly's abuse of the Wave-Form. Their beams leaped across the gulf between the two peaks of the Beast's spine and struck around the retreating marines as they charged into the native scrum.

The natives took exception to this interruption.

The king of the callused brutes roared a battle cry. "Culs, with me!" He leaped from his brawl, where he had smashed two of his four opponents to bits, and soared across the gulf to land among the startled riflemen and wreak havoc.

The riflemen opened fire upon his hide, each beam causing him only to flinch as they sizzled across his calluses. He laughed as the rest of his horde leaped across the space between the peaks and laid into the riflemen with glee.

Now that their enemy had fled, the exoskeleton creatures turned on the marines, who were still darting through them. These things were a little shorter than the Prismath, with wicked blades protruding from their forearms, and they had tall, jagged heads with sunken green eyes.

They looked to their own leader as the fighting died down. Votly assumed it was their leader because his exoskeleton bore a large green crest that almost resembled a crown. The leader looked from their fleeing enemy among the riflemen and back to the marines, considered for a moment, and with a rattling hiss yelled, "Ekelts, attack the newcomers! They are here to steal our gland rights!"

Votly hadn't known this at the time, of course, but what she and her marines had encountered was a territory dispute. The Culs and the Ekelts were war bands fighting over one of the closest glands where the Beast excreted fluids to keep its constantly moving parts cool. As the belligerents were concerned, a third side had just entered the fray. The Ekelt king was happy to let his enemy fight his enemy on the peak, while he and his fighters routed the detachment, trying to sneak past them to the fertile glands they fought over.

This was all incredibly distressing for Votly.

She had just moments before made a daring tactical move to get out of danger.

And now she had inadvertently declared war on two different species.

As the marines fled desperately from their new pursuers— who at least did not have projectile weapons—Votly realised that she *really* needed Mallel to tell her what to do ...

CHAPTER 11

Tara Star

The air began to taste like sodden electricity. Tara didn't know how else to explain it. It was as if one of those Light Wizard circuits had sputtered in the drizzle, and now an aura was emanating from it that had a heavy tang.

Whatever was causing it, it must have been a phenomenon of the gravity reefs.

The gravity reefs were where this world's outskirts crumbled out into the orbiting paths of the other orbiting worlds. Apparently the orbit of this little rock she found herself on was slowly ripping it apart, and the world would soon become a ring of ice and dust encircling the Beast.

And by soon, that probably meant in the next hundred years ...

What that all meant for Tara in the immediate sense was that this quarter of the planet was crumbling and fissuring. Her path out of town and through the grey wastes—fleeing from the Slithmet while pursuing the horde of bounty hunters—was marked by more geysers of yellowy gas from the innards of the planet, and metallic rocks floated daintily into the nether.

Some of the floating chunks of rock were big enough that they supported small buildings. Others, much further up into the expanding field of floating rocks, were large enough to hold whole towns. They were connected by busy gondola lines, crisscrossing like a deranged spider's web, where tethered vessels were pulled along from broken world to broken world.

Their passage was silhouetted by the spinning stars as the planet orbited around the titanic Beast, and in the Beast's shadow they were lit by an assortment of neon lights.

Tara would have stopped to enjoy the sight if it were not for the sound of conflict over the next broken ridge. Checking over her shoulder and finding no pursuing Slithmet, Tara sped up the ridge and was struck by the most chaotic sight.

One of the rock formations in the fissure field beneath the ridge was not quite detached from its mother world. It hung onto the surface for dear life by a worn-down stalactite that burrowed deep into a hissing fissure which spewed yellow gas into the wet, electric air.

Around that large, half-embedded rock, there was an arrangement of creatures laying siege against a lone figure at its top. He ducked between the crags and ridges as he fired back upon his enemies with a prism rifle. It was Captain Mallel.

Tara's heart skipped a beat seeing his strong, dark figure scramble about the rock top in his defence.

"Ah," Tara sighed. Despite the danger he was in, she couldn't help but feel a sense of relief, and ... tranquillity, at seeing him. The Luck Symbioid spiked. "Not now." She pushed the fuzzy, butterfly feeling down and took in the situation.

"You're holding back too, eh?" The sinister, silky voice almost made Tara jump.

The bounty hunter—Cronetta Lesh—stepped up beside her, materialising out of the grey wasteland. Tara *wanted* to jump, but after years of standing next to terrifying people, the urge had dwindled to a minor tremble.

"I've been after a bounty like this before," Tara said nonchalantly. "Fighting more than ten people at once can get distracting, so I'll let them cut each other down to size."

"Hah." Cronetta laughed. "Cute, ten people? You expect me to believe you are capable of such a feat, little girl?"

Heat rose in Tara's chest; no one had spoken to her like that since she was an assassin in training. She rounded on the bounty hunter, hand slipping towards her coat, but found Cronetta staring her down with a playful smile.

"I'm only playing." Cronetta raised her hands in mock surrender and bit her lip with sharp teeth. "You do seem ... experienced."

"Is that why you haven't tried to kill me yet?" Tara said.

"Hah." Cronetta placed a hand on her hip—caressing her coiled rope dart—and rocked away from Tara. "It's because I'm curious. You were skulking around in the saloon with a naked Slithmet. Then another places a bounty against this man, and now here you are all alone ... Maybe you aren't after a bounty after all?" Her eyes flickered to Mallel. "He's putting up quite a fight."

"Knowing him," Tara felt no need to hide the truth; they both had the measure of each other now, "he hasn't even begun yet."

As she said this, Mallel ducked out from cover and fired a beam that struck a bounty hunter with fluttering wings. It whined a high-pitched cry and fell into the fissure to its fiery death. "Come on, you shattered fiends! I haven't even begun yet!"

A fresh group of bounty hunters arrived from across the wastes—presumably hired from another town—and surged down into the tumultuous landscape of craggy, half-floating boulders. Tara quickly realised that they were not just surging to get Mallel, but to battle each other as well, fighting each other in order to claim the bounty on his head.

One of the bounty hunters took aim at Mallel with a complicated-looking firearm—but was struck down from behind. He hit the ground with a deft "Ooft" noise, and his weapon went off. The sparks and flames shot into a nearby geyser of gas and flickered momentarily ... and as the luck tingles travelled down Tara's spine, she had an idea.

"What's your name?" Cronetta cocked her head, her hand slipping by her rope dart again. "I like to remember interesting people after they're dead."

"Well, in that case ..." Tara pulled up her scarf around her mouth, glancing at the battlefield below and making a quick assessment of things. "The name is Tara Star, former Night Assassin and founding member of The New Symbicate ..."

Cronetta's muscles tensed. "I've never heard of them."

"But you know from my voice that they aren't things to be trifled with," Tara said, her voice hardening, her fingers flexing as she inched towards her coat pocket.

"I know danger when I see it." Cronetta's salacious smile flashed and then disappeared as she set her face into a grim expression. "Shall we?" She cocked her head again.

Tara took a steady breath, and the two stood there a moment, eyeing each other as the battle raged down the ridge. " ... Let's get to it!" Tara dropped a smoke bomb and ducked under the violent lash from the rope dart that tore its way through the cloud.

Whistling steam she's fast, Tara thought as she dived headfirst down the ridge and rolled painfully over jagged stones.

She smiled despite herself, reminiscing on her time as an assassin when she and countless others had competed for the Ringleader's head. She made some good friends in that fight, and lost some too. As she steadied her hasty descent, her eyes drifted to Mallel upon the rock. *I will not lose him too.*

Her gaze then drifted down to the jutting piece of rock embedded in the sulphur fissure, and she glanced around the other floating rocks, locking eyes on an abandoned, drifting gondola that hung lazily high over the chaos.

The beginnings of a crazy idea danced across her mind, but it was interrupted as she hit the ground hard and flung a throwing knife at the closest bounty hunter to her. He went down with a pained snarl. Cronetta spat a curse somewhere back above her as she swiped through the dissipating smoke cloud in vexation.

Tara had no time to take stock of the battle anymore, as she sensed Cronetta would be hot on her heels and was a dead shot with her rope dart. She kicked away another bounty hunter and dashed through the melee towards the rock where Mallel was making his stand.

A thug rushed her rear and was cut down by a beam from Mallel's pistol. *So he did see my smoke.*

Tara dived over a low swipe from a bendy, gangly stem of a creature and crash tackled into it, driving her blade into its … well … into what she thought was its neck. It did the job, though; the thing did not get back up. She growled, jumping from the fresh corpse and spin-kicking one of the blob-like aliens who was wielding a club.

A whip crack caught her attention.

She spun as Cronetta lashed out with a rope dart—she had entered the fray and was in hot pursuit of Tara—whatever her original intention was, it was clear she saw Tara as a viable threat to her bounty. The rope ripped at the eyes of a hapless mercenary who was trading potshots with Mallel, and with a hard yank the dart flicked down with a spray of green blood and knocked the barrel of the mercenary's weapon down to fire on Tara.

With her honed reflexes Tara ducked and rolled behind cover as a blast of red chunks expelled from the rifle and littered the free-for-all brawl around her with burning shrapnel. The embattled bounty hunters and mercenaries cried out as Tara produced another smoke bomb, which she set off without hesitation.

The purple smoke hissed and was carried on the air currents spurting from the fissures, filling the already foggy battlefield with opaque confusion. Cronetta hissed in frustration and charged into the murky fray, whipping her rope dart around her at the ready, to use on anyone who lurched out of the din.

Tara could have taken this moment to engage Cronetta, but the fray was too tumultuous, too chaotic, with too many involved parties. Instead she turned and sighted her goal. She pulled another bomb from her coat pocket and eyed the fissure spurting yellow smoke from the incision point of Mallel's bastion.

The air was combustible; she had noticed when the less disciplined bounty hunters fired near the spurts of gas. Concentrated below the surface, that combustion could aid her next move.

"Here goes." Tara pulled a fuse from another pocket and threaded it into the bomb in her hands. She lit the fuse and tossed it at the base of the boulder. It clattered past the spewing fissure and tumbled into the ominous yellow depths.

"What was that?" A bounty hunter was about to strike her down but hesitated at her action.

Tara shot him a devilish grin. "An incendiary bomb." Then she punched the bounty hunter in the face.

She shot out of the smoke cloud and bolted for the base of the boulder. As Tara leaped up the wall, scurrying over the nooks and crags to scramble up the uneven surface, a gunshot struck the rock beside her. She ignored it. She only had a minute to get to *relative* safety.

Tara reached the top of the listing boulder and popped over the edge. Mallel turned, drawing his cutlass and hesitating when he recognised her silhouette in the choked air.

"Miss Star," his stern voice broke for just a moment, "I thought that was your smoke bomb."

Tara dashed in and wrapped her arms around him before she realised what she was doing. "Ah ..." She leaned back, patting Mallel down, pretending to check for injuries. "You seem to be in one piece."

"Ah ..." he returned, "you seem to be in fine shape ... I mean, fine fighting shape too."

A shot pinged out over his shoulder—breaking their revelry—and they ducked. "Do you know where my crew is?"

"The loyal ones or the traitors?" Tara asked.

"Both." Mallel fired at another flying attacker; this one was gliding rather than buzzing, and its corpse slammed into the wall of the boulder with a crunch.

"No."

"Shards, do you have a pla ..." He drew his cutlass and activated the power as a scuttling creature scrambled over the lip of the boulder.

What happened next seemed an unfortunate occurrence, but Tara's Luck Symbioid flared so strongly, she flinched.

As the power surged through the cutlass, it vibrated uncontrollably and ripped out of Mallel's hands, clinging to the rock. A piece of rock sprung out from the point of impact, soaring over Tara as she flinched from the intense tingling, and the rock struck the scuttling creature in the face. It tumbled back over the edge with a keening cry.

"Cogrust," Tara swore as she pulled herself back up onto her feet. "That sword was one of our best weapons against the Slithmet."

"It can still work." Mallel gripped the cutlass and turned it off as he pulled it from the stone. "Just as a regular sword."

Tara drew her combat knife. "Nothing wrong with a regular blade, Captain. Now defend this point and hold on—we're about to go for a ride!"

Below in the brawl, Cronetta leaped off a rock, rolled between the legs of a lumbering beast, and came up running, spinning her rope dart around her to keep other foes at bay while sprinting for the boulder. She knew that Tara had thrown something into the fissure, and she had a pretty good idea of what that little upstart's plan was to escape. She struck out, letting her rope dart fly and embed into the rocky surface as Tara's incendiary bomb went off.

Upon the rock, as the Luck Symbioid flared in warning, Tara rushed to tackle Mallel down and pin him in place. They locked eyes, their breath in each other's faces as the world lit up in brilliant light. Beneath the fissure, the bomb exploded, and the fiery contents ignited the churning gasses that rushed upwards in a geyser of flames. The battlefield was engulfed in the explosion, and the rocky bastion was ejected, hurtling through the gravity reefs like a lobbed stone.

Mallel's powerful arms encircled Tara as the sodden, tangy air rushed past them, changing into dry, tangy air when they left the little world's field of fissures and jettisoned into the network of mini worlds and gondola lines.

Tara wrenched Mallel's cutlass from his hand as the air rushed past them like a hurricane and scrambled up onto a protruding rock. She aimed the cutlass at the closest tether while they hurtled through the network, hoping against hope that her idea would work. She braced herself, tensing all of the muscles in her body, and turned the cutlass on.

It was immediately stricken, about to be wrenched from her grip by the electromagnetic forces going haywire around her. But she kept her resolve, straining to keep the sword pointed up towards the nearest tether, which bent towards them as they flew past, drawn to the magnetic resonance of the sword in the chaotic miasma of forces.

The tether curved within reaching distance, and Tara screamed, wrenching the cutlass down to ground level and drawing the tether in closer, close enough to be drawn to the sword. She let go and rolled back; the cable latched onto the sword, which latched onto the rocky ground, and the boulder became entangled, spinning around the tether in a cyclone.

Tara slipped, falling over the side of the ridge, only for Mallel to reach out and grip her by the arm. He grimaced and held onto her for dear life, and Tara could do nothing but watch the cosmos spin as their little rock whirled around the tether uncontrollably.

Eventually, the violent tornado slowed, the worlds stopped spinning around the rock—at least they stopped spinning violently—and Tara was hauled over the edge by Mallel.

"That was brilliant," Mallel said, breathlessly.

"That was insane!" she replied.

They sprawled to rest on their little makeshift gondola, which now drifted between the gravity reefs, unaware of a third passenger that had secured themselves to the bottom of the vessel.

* * *

Cronetta pulled herself to where her rope dart had embedded in the bottom of the expelled rock. Her hat and coat were singed from the explosion, but she was very much alive. As she gripped the rock with her hands, she turned back to the little world below her, which was shrinking away.

The battlefield was a smouldering ruin. The Slithmet's war band was roasted, and the bounty hunters who had survived were picking themselves up and limping back to town to drown their sorrows. But two Slithmet were perched upon the ridge.

Cronetta pulled a signal light from her coat and flashed it towards them, and even from this distance she could make out their eyes flashing red in response. The signal was clear to them: they had an agent pursuing their bounty, and she expected to be paid when she delivered.

The two Slithmet on the surface eyed one another. One grinned wickedly as the other licked its metallic lips.

"Will your new exosuit keep up, Hoztic?" one said. "It was the best I could do on short notice."

"It will suffice," Hoztic hissed. "That upstart Symbicate brat means to get to the skull. The Beast is already on course to destroy her world, but to take over it and ensure the Rel's plan succeeds, we need to get there before her."

"I suggest we pursue her then. That tether can only lead to one place, and we can head them off before they make a plan to get ahead of us."

"What about the skull?" Hoztic asked.

"I have war bands converging on it from every chit-driven despot in these forsaken worlds. Our people battling the Custanguin will be reinforced by cutthroats soon enough, not even realising that it will be their own throats they're cutting." His companion cackled.

Hoztic looked down at his new, wicked-sharp talons and flexed them. "Very well then. Lead the way. Our new bounty hunter friend will signal us when we get closer, and then I'm going to skin the symbioids right out of that miscreant's spine!"

CHAPTER 12

Snipes

Snipes sat upon the crest of what would be described as a ridge in any ordinary landscape, except this landscape was more than ordinary—extraordinary, one might say. The descent dwindled into a yawning, cavernous abyss that shifted and undulated with pulsing, technicoloured waves of electromagnetic brilliance. The show of light shimmered off the fleshy innards and metallic structure of the great Beast he now found himself within.

The churning depths rumbled, pools of fizzing, hissing stuff slopped against sinewy shores, and Snipes felt his own stomach churn, twist, drop, and rise all at the same time. He gripped the prism rifle in his hands and took a deep breath.

The village of strange people was behind him. Flayr, his lover—now client—was in their hands. All there was for him to do now was to descend into the unknown chaos, into the belly of the Beast.

He took another breath, deeper this time, ignoring the acrid scent that made the bile rise within him, and considered his new weapon.

The prism set into the end of the barrel was cracked, although Snipes had to squint to see it. The lights that blinked and shone through the mechanisms were dulled, as if seeping from the hairline fracture. That would—Snipes assumed—lessen the power the gun could bring to bear. He had seen rifles like this sear through the twisted sinews of the Rel husks back in Copper Cobble, yet it had only inconvenienced this cancer he now had to do battle with, this Infyrra.

I have to find my blunderbuss.

He patted the ammo pouch in the webbing under his coat. His shots from his revolvers seemed to do more damage to the thing than the prism weapons. They warbled its skin. If he could only find his gun and unload a flechette bundle round or two into the creature, he might disorient it enough to kill it ... *Might.*

All this was a moot point, however. Snipes had no idea where to find the creature; all he knew to do was to descend into the depths and let it find him. At least it would distract the Infyrra from the villagers for a time, and he might find clues as to where the *Motebeam* crashed. *That kid did say it ricocheted down this way.*

Sick of hesitating, Snipes stepped over the precipice. His foot immediately sank into moosh, and Snipes's innards recoiled in terror. This ground had no purchase. He could not find solid footing; he could not take a shot with any accuracy.

He bit down on his rising anxiety. He could do this. There simply wasn't any other choice.

With trepidation adding resistance to every step, Snipes marched into the fleshy marshes, which glistened with each cylindrical pulse of light from the Beast's body. Each footfall squelched into the spongy texture of tissue, and moisture seeped into the seams of his worn boots.

Further down there was a spinelike protrusion which loomed ominously from the fleshy marshes in the rhythmic lighting. Snipes could not help but feel a strong sense of foreboding, but it was solid at least. He could make ground there for a while as he rallied his courage.

He clambered onto the jutting *rock*—for lack of a better word—and scanned the descending steppe. Pink, viscous gunk marked the stones and debris as the slope continued into darkness. The Infyrra had left scraps of itself, and Snipes realised he would have to keep surging into the bowels to follow the trail.

It took some time, though Snipes had no idea how to mark the passing of a day—all there was in terms of light was the pulsating flash that travelled down the Beast as it swam through the ether. Every few minutes the pulse would repeat, which lulled Snipes into a fugue state as he marched deeper into the guts. As he descended further, tubes and nodules and sinew crowded the area like foliage. They pumped and squelched and twitched like animated roots and branches in an alien swamp. But other than the repetitive, squelching thrum and the deep boom of a heartbeat somewhere, Snipes found himself in silence.

"You really got yourself into it this time," he said.

"Oh?" An eyeball popped up from a porous part of the bone he marched down, and Snipes all but screamed, jumping back and pointing his prism rifle at the newcomer. "Hold fire. You've been walking over my home for quite some time, stranger!" the eyeball said. "What business have you here in the belly?"

"I'm hunting a cancer?" Snipes felt foolish saying it aloud. "The Infyrra."

"Oh, then may I eat your corpse once it's done with you?" The eyeball cocked as if it was cocking its head. Snipes could not tell where the voice was coming from; it was a husky, wheezy thing, and he decided that he had no need to see the mouth that produced it.

"Just tell me where to go," Snipes said.

The eyeball gestured over the side of an approaching ridge that slanted down into a pool of hissing green liquid. "Down there is a heat vent, very steamy. The Infyrra likes to stay there sometimes to hydrate. But be warned, many Custanguin have ventured there to battle it. They don't take kindly to ..." The eyeball looked him up and down. "... foreigners. You may find yourself fighting more than the Infyrra." The eyeball made a smacking sound. Snipes couldn't help but imagine below the bone there was something licking its lips.

"I'll try to avoid other interested parties," Snipes said. "Thank you."

"Oh no, thank you. Just try to preserve as much of your flesh as possible. It's been a while since I've eaten something soft."

"I'll do my best." Snipes grimaced and marched over to the side of the ridge which led into a steaming ravine. The taste of bile made him swallow, but he realised in horror that it was not his own bile that he was tasting, but the Beast's. It was in the steam; it was in the air ... His heart rebelled as his feet left the bony ridge and sunk into the fleshy moosh once more. "I'll do my best," he said again, gripping his weapon tightly.

The Hired Hero waded into the murky, steam-hissing, squelch-ridden cesspool of whatever the cogrusted Perversity this land was. The air was damp and muggy, clinging to his skin and his garments, condensing against the brass components of his armour and the chrome plating of his Light Wizard rifle, equipment sourced from both his home world and that of Prisma.

It was a constant slog. Every step into mildly corrosive, ankle-deep water caused Snipes to suppress a yelp as he leaped back in fright, but he carried on. Eventually a shape loomed out of the green-grey depths, something foreign—like everything here, he supposed—with jagged edges that towered over Snipes's puny form.

He inched closer to its base, nudging it with the prism set into the barrel of his rifle. It did not budge. Whatever it was, it was dead. Snipes scrambled back to a protruding bit of half-digested rock, scrambling over it to get a better look at the inert corpse before him. Snipes was shocked to realise the shape was humanoid-ish. It looked like some armoured defender.

"That's a Custanguin."

Snipes yelped and spun, aiming his weapon at the little eyeball stalk that plopped out from the stomach swamps.

"Cogrust!" Snipes swore. "What in the Three Perversities are you?"

"I'm a helper; I help break down the matter that the Great One can't digest from what it eats."

"Such as?"

"Organic things mostly. *Don't* look at me like that! By this point it's all usually long dead. I would never, and I mean *never* eat a living creature ... except for this one time there was this little bug-like thing that was quite hardy until I accidentally chewed on it ... Anyway, that's unimportant. This Custanguin was a good chap. That Infyrra, though, it came in and folded into every crevice of this beautiful defender here until it couldn't move, sucking out all of the spongy goodness to add to its own mass. When the Custanguin kills something, at least it breaks down its foe into something the people around here can use. But this Infyrra, it shares nothing with the ecosystem it resides in; it just consumes, consumes, consumes, and gives nothing back!

"It didn't help that the Custanguin were already weakened from the drought. News says the Great One swam away from the nebula clouds and into some barren patch of the void. Who knows why, though?"

"Well," Snipes gazed up at the defender, the Custanguin, "my little eyeball friend. I'm going to stop it." *Somehow.* "Hopefully I can find my friend's ship before it gets me. Maybe then we can bring our cannons to bear."

"Cannons?" the eyeball said.

"Yeah, big guns." Snipes patted the rifle in his hands.

"Ah, you're some kind of ... heavy weapons expert?"

"No, I'm a sniper ... I take precise shots from a distance. I am very much out of my element here. But I have a job to do. This prism rifle here can sear the cancer and make it recoil; bigger ones will do more damage. But what I really need is my own blunderbuss. It's modified to take crack shots, and I can alter the munitions if I need to. A solid projectile seemed to confuse the thing more than a beam. I have my pistols, of course, but they use smaller rounds, and it may not be enough."

"Well, here is your chance to figure it out." The eyeball darted around. "It's coming this way."

"Where?" Snipes scanned the hissing haze frantically, and then turned back to the eyeball, which had receded into the acrid waters without so much as a splash. "Cogrust."

The atmosphere seemed to change, and the steam warbled with the rumbling approach of something sickly. Another shape loomed in the suffocating dimness, not angular and jutting like the dead guardian that stood stoically in the swamps. This creature was round and viscous.

Snipes raised his rifle at the dark shape and tracked it as it rolled and sloshed through the uneven ground like a gelatinous landslide. It shuddered as it bumped into the Custanguin; the horrid rumbling of the thing keened throughout the hissing landscape, and Snipes felt his stomach sag.

"Enough of this." He squeezed the trigger.

The sizzling beam erupted from the prism rifle, hissing off the damp air as it illuminated a horrid shape in the distance. The cancerous beast rumbled in agony, and despite having no discernible features, it *turned* on Snipes, homing in on the thing that caused it pain.

In the brief flash of light, Snipes was reminded of the battle at Copper Cobble. This creature possessed trace strands of black sinew within its pink mass; it had been influenced by the Rel. The Rel had done something to this Beast, he realised, and in doing so—altering its path perhaps to fly towards their sun well—it had wreaked untold calamity on the people who lived here.

Snipes gritted his teeth; this plague *had* to be stopped.

He wiped sweat from his brow and fired another beam. The Infyrra roared and charged towards him. "I thought it would run away from the pain!" Snipes cursed and dived from the little ridge he stood upon, slinging the rifle over his shoulder and reaching for the inert appendage of the Custanguin.

The Infyrra slammed into the ridge a fraction after Snipes leaped away. Horrid pink folds engulfed the rocky protrusion. Snipes clambered up the arm of the Custanguin and ascended onto its crown, pulling out his rifle to fire again.

A tendril lashed out from the Infyrra. It was something with strange, sticky feelers that slapped at the barrel, latching on to it and tearing it from Snipes's hands. It almost tore him from his perch atop the strange corpse as well.

"Cogrust!

The rifle clattered into the churning folds of the Infyrra as it swarmed the corpse of the Custanguin, surging up to gloop and paw at Snipes's coat as he drew his two pistols.

He fired quick, precise shots into the reaching tendrils, each shot hitting their mark and sending vibrating warbles down the thing's skin, which caused it to hesitate. The ripples shimmered down its body, dispersing as if a pebble had been thrown into a large pond. As the ripples crisscrossed and folded over one another, one of the folds parted to reveal the butt of the prism rifle.

Snipes cursed again, and the butt sank deeper into the hungry flesh of the Infyrra as it rallied and started surging up to him again.

There was only one way he was going to escape this encounter, with that very prism rifle, and there was only one way to get it ... to give up his solid ground and dive into the churning mass.

Snipes did not have time to think nor fret. The first tendril lashed around his ankle, and with a scream of horrid dread he opened fire. Not precisely this time, not sure, calculated shots. Instead he closed his eyes and fired wildly, emptying the chambers of his pistols, sending ripple upon disrupting ripple across the Infyrra as it bayed and shrunk back. And Snipes, still screaming, followed.

He leaped from the head of the Custanguin and dived headfirst into the churning, dilapidated mass. Holstering one pistol in the chaos, he reached out, his fingers caressing the butt of the rifle as it, the creature, and he fell into the acid swamps of the belly.

Snipes found himself amid a churning broil of adhesive mess, his world going dark as the devouring flesh absorbed him. It recoiled as the stomach acids from the wider belly seeped into its innards and stung the Infyrra, which keened in pain—unprotected on the *inside*—as Snipes gripped the butt of his weapon.

While the darkness closed in, Snipes pulled the rifle close. The caustic pain from the Infyrra and the Beast's stomach acids layered over his skin, and he pulled the trigger.

In the darkness, there was suddenly light.

The beam of the prism rifle seared through the churning darkness, and the Infyrra screamed again. It ripped away from the source of the pain as quickly as it could and retreated, ejecting Snipes into the acidic pools.

Panting and shivering, he pushed himself out of the slow-burning acid pools and up onto the lip of a jutting bone as the Infyrra lumbered back into the hissing dimness.

The eyeball returned. "You fought off the Infyrra."

An ominous growl reverberated down the belly.

"But it will be back." Snipes choked.

He picked himself up and dashed down the Beast's digestive tract. His breath was in his throat with a rising bile as the realities of what he had just done came crashing into his awareness, along with one key detail.

As he squeezed the trigger, as he gave his final act to escape from the flesh of the Infyrra, he saw another weapon slowly dissolving in the belly of that thing. His own rifle, his modified blunderbuss, it could keep the beast at bay longer than his prism rifle or his pistols ... he would have to enter it again before it could dissolve his weapon ... or he would never reach the *Motebeam* alive.

And he realised, too, that the thing routed only after it was attacked from *inside*. Snipes shivered to think of what he now had to do to complete his mission.

The Infyrra roared and surged back out of the steaming depths. Snipes ducked and dashed, continuing down the tract as the eyeball *helper* squealed and sunk away.

As Snipes reached the end of the tract, he found a conduit which sloped downwards, running with flowing digested matter. Snipes steeled himself and dived down it as the Infyrra slammed into the small opening, quaking the whole area as Snipes tumbled and fell through churning, caustic darkness.

Votly

From one pursuing enemy to another.

The Ekelts, these wraith-like exoskeleton tribal warriors, tore across the spire-scape like rapids crashing over one another to vie for a swipe against Votly and her warriors.

Curla pulled Votly over a ridge and turned to fire with her pistol at the closest of the strange foe. The beam tore from her weapon and smacked right in its skull plate. Its head snapped back under the force, and the beam fractured into a violent spark. The creature slowly leered back, eerie eye slits blinking away the confounding experience before it snarled.

"These things have armour against our guns!" Curla clobbered the thing, which knocked it back, for the moment.

Votly felt her stomach lurch. Gazing up at the changing skies, she could make out the orbs and dust fields of the orbiting worlds. They swung into view as the Beast's body folded, taking its next magnetic stroke through the void.

"Are they stronger than us?" Votly asked.

Balt grunted as he butted back another, the sharp appendages on its wrists missing his chest by a hair's breadth. "Hard to say. They're persistent, though." He fired a beam at the next creature. In its temporary bewilderment, Balt surged forward and shoulder-charged it off the rise.

"Then we hold here for a moment!" Votly ordered, swiping through the display on her Light Gauntlet. The marines formed a tight circle on the ridge as it rose higher into the sky. "Hold the high ground while it lasts. This is the peak we needed to get to. I'll try and get a message off … I can see Mallel's beacon pulsing weakly!"

"Make it count," Curla barked, kicking back another of the things, her boot crunching against its exoskeleton. "We can break their armour with brute force, but our beams only confound them for a moment."

"Aye!" A marine drew his energy cutlass and made to switch it on before Curla barked at him not to. "Right, wouldn't work." He swiped with the inert blade, but in his momentary hesitation, the Ekelt warrior got close enough to gore him with its wrist scythes. He died with a scream before the lucky beast was mobbed by two of the marine's compatriots.

Votly ignored the horrible scream and the cries of anguish from the other marines, typing out commands on her Light Gauntlet, hoping against hope that her signal would reach Mallel.

"Come in, come in, Captain Mallel!" she cried into her gauntlet as the sound of a clattering and violent melee enclosed their position. The marines were making their desperate last stand. "Captain!" Her voice broke.

There was a hiss of static and strange blips and beeps of interference as the signal struggled to compete with the Beast's magnetosphere, and a voice finally broke through.

"Votly?" The voice was deep, powerful, commanding, wonderful.

"Captain! Yes, it's Votly! I'm marooned on the spine of the Beast with a squadron of marines. We were pursued by the riflemen, but now we've stumbled into some kind of territorial war among the natives."

"Can you get away from them?" Another voice cut in, Tara's.

"Tara!" Votly cried. "I don't know. We're cut off and surrounded."

"Listen, Votly," Mallel said, "the Rel already set this Beast on a course with our worlds. There's a *chance* that the Beast won't attack Prisma and Stemcog without more intervention from the Rel, but we can't hope for that. How long do we have until it reaches them?"

"Days if we're lucky." Votly furrowed her brow as she tried to remember all of the dozens of calculations flying through her mind. "After the Wave-Form explosion scattered us around the place ... perhaps just one day given our luck."

"Even less." Tara's voice garbled over the radio wave. "The Slithmet know we're trying to stop the Beast. They'll be pursuing us to the opening we made in the skull. We need to get there before they do, but it's going to be a war zone by all accounts."

"Votly," Mallel said evenly, "we'll need backup."

Votly gazed skullwards in desperation; they had started off up that way and had slowly been pushed back under fire from riflemen and now these native things. "Captain, we … I can't get through."

"Votly." Mallel's voice was hard, but kind. "Scrond believed in you. I do too."

Votly swallowed a lump in her throat. "I'll make it to the skull, Captain, I promise you."

"You're a Light Wizard, Votly!" Tara's voice chimed in. "You've got this!"

"Yes," she said. "We'll get to the skull, no matter what it takes."

"Good girl," Mallel said. "We'll meet you there, I have no doubt. Any idea on where our ship is?" The transmission became fuzzy and hard to hear.

"I have no idea, sir. It might be *inside* the Beast, but I can't confirm that. Since I landed we haven't had a chance to catch our breath!"

Mallel's reply was too charged with static for Votly to make out. She desperately adjusted settings and readings on her gauntlet to isolate the signal, but it eventually winked out.

"Captain! Captain!" she cried. But the line was dead. She toggled a switch on her gauntlet, repeating the broadcasted conversation on the *Motebeam's* frequency. If it managed to get within range, any surviving crew would know where to go, and why.

"What's our plan?" Curla cried.

"We need to go back the way we came!" Votly said. "Mallel says this thing is going to be manipulated to attack our world. We need to get to the skull to help him stop it."

"Shards, that's insane!" Balt said.

"It's the captain's orders!"

"Fine," Balt spat. "Lads, ladettes, get ready to make a push!"

"Has your mind broken into shards?" a marine cradling his bleeding shoulder cried. "We're barely holding on as it is!"

"We've been reactive until now." Votly set her voice hard, her captain's resolve surging through her. *Shards, he is a good leader.* "Now *we're* the ones taking action."

Something in her voice stifled the retort building in the marine.

"Now, fix your bayonets." Votly fired a beam at a rising Ekelt, and the snap of light sent it tumbling back into its companions, "The captain needs us to charge skullwards, and we're going to push through anything that gets in our way!"

"You heard the lady!" Curla barked, fixing her energy knife to her prism rifle, but refraining from switching the power on. "We're gonna brute force our way outta this mess like we shoulda done from the start!"

There was a rippling clatter as the other marines who were able fixed their blades to the barrels of their rifles.

"Now," Votly barked before the strength left her resolve, "for Prisma, the *Motebeam*, and Captain Mallel!"

Votly was moving before she realised what she was doing. She surged over the ridge, kicking out at the skull plate of a startled Ekelt and charging over its tumbling form as—to her bewilderment—the marines at her back echoed her war cry and charged out past her.

They formed a wedge, ploughing through the Ekelt natives, who were caught completely unprepared for the counterattack from the prism marines. Their bladed rifles fractured the bony exo-plates that protected their enemy's bodies, and the marines carried on surging through them.

The Ekelt king—the one with the green-tinged crest protruding from its brow—snarled with razor-sharp teeth as Votly surged towards it. It reared to slash at her, and Votly's eyes went wide, her adrenaline shrivelling to some dark place within her as she realised she was the tip of the spear in a brutal melee, about to be diced to pieces in a foolish fit of aggression.

As her life flashed before her eyes, a bayonet shot past her ear from behind and flashed. Curla fired at point-blank range, a shot that ricocheted off the king's crest, and it tumbled back with a startled cry. And with that, the marines had broken through.

Votly found the rolling spire-scape before her, the Beast's skull rocking in and out of sight in the distant horizon as it swam through the void. "Onwards, marines, to the skull of the Beast!"

"Aye!" Balt sounded. "Into hell and out again, lads and ladettes!"

Votly risked a look over her shoulder. The marines had rallied well and had broken through the mass of scythes that was their new enemy. The Ekelts scrambled in their wake to pursue the marines back up the skull. She allowed herself to hope—they had done it. She glanced at Balt, who smiled at her, a nasty gash seeping blue blood from his cheek, and she risked a smile back.

A beam of light struck him in the chest, searing through his thick coat and knocking him flat on his back.

Votly gasped, looking back towards the skull to find the source of the beam.

A surge of brown rolled over the next ridge—the riflemen—and they were accompanied by a horde of the calloused, fleshy brutes—the Culs.

"They've formed an alliance!" Curla cried. "But how?"

They killed Balt ... The thought seeped across Votly's mind in a stunned motion.

The marines took cover under the crevices and ridges of the Beast's spine as the Ekelts surged up behind them. Votly realised that this was probably the end; she gazed at Balt's body, inert in the ephemeral, magnetic dust, and gripped her pistol tightly. One of the Ekelts was tripped up by a beam that struck it from the riflemen side, and she had an idea.

"They're attacking both of us ..." Votly realised. "We can do the same!"

"What?" Curla said under a furrowed brow.

"King Ekelt!" Votly screamed while the Ekelts fumbled under the volley from the riflemen. It snapped its head her way as it took cover. "Good," Votly said to herself. "It can understand me ..." She yelled over the din, over the rumbling of the ground beneath her that signalled the approaching horde of Culs. "Our enemies and yours have joined forces to destroy you. Help us destroy them, or we will both die here."

The king's beady green eyes darted between her and the charging army ahead of them. It narrowed its eyes on her finally and nodded, letting out a bone-rending screech that sounded vaguely like an order. Votly strained to understand what it was saying.

"Kill the Culs! Kill the brown cloaks! The greys will aid us until it is time for us to fight again!"

"Figures." Votly rolled her eyes, gritted her teeth, and popped over the ridge to fire into the oncoming Culs, whose advance was supported by the riflemen firing potshots behind them.

"Just another day as a marine, lads!" Curla barked. "Let's shatter their resolve!"

CHAPTER 14

Tara Star

The sounds out here were odd, muted, yet they echoed around the drifting gravity reefs of sparkling dust and ice that encircled the immense Beast. Every twang of the tether sent a note of music that reverberated throughout the vast space.

Tara sat upon a boulder on the upper ridge of the little meteor they were riding to their next destination. Light from distant stars reflected off the ice, glistening like a frozen sunrise over the ocean. Beams of light from the sun danced around the magnetic eddies produced by the Beast's gentle motion.

"It's lovely, isn't it?" Mallel wrangled with the tether to fix their makeshift gondola on a more or less straight path towards the next port. It was no longer bound by his brimming cutlass; instead it was fed through a jerry-rigged contraption Mallel had cobbled together from old scraps found on the asteroid. He was a sailor, after all.

Tara did not react. She had known Mallel was watching her delight in the sights; she had known, and struggled to pretend not to notice. "It's like, like … it's like a dream world."

"Dream worlds." Mallel sat stiffly next to her and allowed his gaze to be torn from her face to trace the shapes that the light made through the dust. "There are many here, with many more varied people than we could have ever predicted …" He hummed in thought, his voice growing deep.

Tara tried not to focus on the depths his hum reached. "You're worried that if we destroy this Beast to protect our home worlds, it will destroy the innocents here."

Mallel's hum caught in his throat. "Yes."

"And yet, you plan to kill the Beast anyway?"

"What else is there to do, Miss Star? It's our worlds or theirs."

"My symbioid, the Master Symbioid, I can use it."

"How?" Mallel regarded her sternly, but not unkindly.

"I don't know." Tara wrapped her coat tight and turned away from him. "I'm still not sure entirely how it works."

"What else is there to do, Miss Star?" Mallel asked again.

"Is that what you asked yourself before you opened fire on Crankod?" She shivered as she said it.

Mallel did not answer.

"I didn't know there was another way," he finally said.

She turned to face him. "But there was! And there might be another way here."

"You don't know that," Mallel retorted. "Our worlds hang in the balance."

"And so do theirs." Tara gestured to the vast network of orbiting planets. "What good is it to vanquish evil and preserve life if we become evil ourselves, if we vanquish life ourselves?"

Mallel sighed through his teeth. "It's not that simple this time. We're scattered, cut off, outnumbered, and this creature swims ever onwards to our worlds. You would risk your people to protect it? You would stop me from becoming a monster at the expense of Thomas, Billie, and Eleanor?"

"You don't have to be a monster, Mallel. I used to think you did to survive in this world …" she looked around, "… in these worlds. But it's just not true. You are a good man. Make the harder choice here."

Mallel was silent for another moment. "Let's just get to the skull for starters, Miss Star. It's likely we won't even survive that far, and this argument would be a moot point."

Tara nodded to herself. "Very well. In the meantime, you know you can just call me Tara, right?"

Mallel nodded. "I know." His gaze drifted back to meet hers, the stars reflecting in his deep, dark eyes.

The Luck Symbioid spiked, sending shivers down her spine, and she turned away. "I told you to keep back."

"Oh," Mallel shifted back, "forgive me…"

"No, no, not you, the Luck Symbioid. It keeps flaring."

"And you wish it not to?" Mallel asked. "It is a great asset, a part of you; perhaps it is the reason you still live."

"And what choice did I have in those matters?" Tara spat. "It wove with me without my consent, as did the Master Symbioid. Hoztic was right … and ever since then I have lived through battles where people close to me have died. Do you know how I killed the man who was originally woven with the Luck Symbioid?"

"No."

"He was shooting at me, laughing, mocking; I didn't want to kill him. But I realised that for him to get what he wanted, I had to *not get* what I wanted ... I just wanted to leave ... I didn't want to kill him. The luck was fickle that day..."

"So it seems you used the symbioid before it even wove with your body," Mallel tutted. "Have you considered it was you who used it without its consent first?"

Tara shot him an angry look.

"I only say," Mallel raised his hands placatingly, "that the two of you—the three of you—are now one. Perhaps that is not such a bad thing, to have a union like that?"

"I survived," Tara said, "and people around me died instead."

"Ah, I see." Mallel sighed. "I know what that is like."

Tara made to retort but held her tongue. She knew of the horrors he faced when the Rel invaded Prisma. He was a leader and warrior through necessity, not desire. Perhaps he would have been a more gentle man in another life; perhaps she would have ...

"You have gifts, Tara," Mallel said, interrupting her thoughts. "Gifts many would kill for. I wager you and you alone can wield them to the benefit of all where others initially failed ..."

"So would you trust me to simply stop the Beast if it comes to it? Even if it means you giving up a chance to kill it?"

He looked at her, hard.

"Because," Tara hesitated, "I wouldn't want us to come to blows."

"Tara," Mallel said, "I ..."

The Luck Symbioid spiked, a different spike than the one prompting her to act on her impulse to just lean in and kiss the man. This one was a warning. Danger was close by ...

"Tara?" Mallel sensed her tension, his hand slipping to his hip holster beneath his thick coat.

Tara spirited up from the stone, her gaze darting this way and that across the barren fissure-expelled rock they were using as a raft through the gravity reefs. As she slipped from where she was sitting, the whistle of a blade cut through the dense air, followed by the lightning crack of a whip.

A rope dart arched out from beneath Tara's perch and snapped around to slam into her previous seat, the dart embedding into the shale-like rock and lodging in place. Tara's eyes went wide in recognition. Cronetta was here.

With a grunt, Cronetta launched out from her perch underneath the little makeshift gondola. In the ebbing flows of different gravitational pulls, she arched out from the little raft, up, and swung high over the top of Mallel and Tara as they drew their weapons. With another grunt Cronetta yanked the rope dart free from its penetration of the shale stone and landed with a muted clamour, the dart spiriting back to her before she caught it single-handed.

"Howdy." She smiled, flicking the rim of her large hat with her index finger. "I believe, little bounty hunter, you have something that belongs to me." Her hungry eyes flickered to Mallel and back to Tara. She homed in on Tara's stirring rage, and her smile turned into a wicked grin, intensified by her elongated features. "Oh sweet child, he *will* belong to me."

Tara made to step between Mallel and Cronetta, but found him stepping forward alongside of her … ready to fight as her equal. "She is no child," Mallel said evenly. "She is a warrior, and you will find out that warriors do not give up so easily." His pistol was drawn, and he levelled it at Cronetta.

"Oh, a warrior now, is she? First she was just a patron hiding in the Jaunt Saloon, then a bounty hunter, then a bodyguard. It seems she can't make up her mind what she wants," Cronetta hissed. "Perhaps she should decide before I decide for her." She looked over her shoulder at where the makeshift gondola was heading, towards a derelict little port town on a floating chunk of rock.

"And what would you decide for me?" Tara asked, starting to circle around Cronetta as Mallel mirrored her movements.

"Chaos!" Cronetta spun and whipped her rope dart at the crude fixing of the tether to the asteroid. With a whip crack the tether snapped loose, and the boulder careened wildly towards the little port town.

Tara wasted no time, already lobbing a throwing knife at Cronetta's exposed back. Ready for the counterattack, Cronetta ripped back her rope dart and spun it with the cord in her hands to deflect Tara's knife, then the next one, and the next.

"Stop lobbing knifes so I can get a shot in!" Mallel shouted.

Oh yeah, he has a pistol … Tara thought, feeling foolish.

She ducked back so Mallel could get a cleaner shot. Cronetta slashed at the ground before her, kicking up a slow-motion wave of dust that radiated out from her in the ebbing gravity currents. Mallel fired, and the beam of light struck the magnetic particles and dissipated across the impromptu wall like lightning illuminating a distant cloud. The rope dart shot out from the makeshift shield as the light died and struck Mallel in the hand.

With a gasp he dropped his prism pistol and drew his cutlass instead.

Cronetta burst through the dispersing debris field she had created—tearing a silhouette through it before the granules and particles drifted back into one another—and she cackled as she spun the rope dart in her hands. "I didn't think this job would be so thrilling!"

Tara charged in, rolling under the follow-up strike that Cronetta whipped around her head, and she leaped high to fly-kick her in the face. Cronetta ducked to one side, and Tara sailed past her. Mallel was there next, lunging with his blade and sniping Cronetta's hand. Cronetta dodged and spun and lashed out with her rope dart as fast as lightning. The cord lashed around Mallel's sword arm, and the two were locked in a long-distance grapple. Cronetta tried to pull him in closer as Mallel tried to release himself from her snare.

Tara had recovered by this point, spinning to find the two combatants locked in struggle. "Good," Tara said under her breath. "She's distracted."

Her tingling flared.

Tara looked up; the derelict port was hurtling towards them. Or, more accurately, they were hurtling towards it.

"Cogrust!" Tara's heart sank as her adrenaline spiked.

The port grew larger with each passing second. The tingling of the Luck Symbioid rose in her heart. "Save Mallel too!" she willed, with all of her heart. "I don't want you to just benefit me!"

The tingling spiked like a rash was spreading throughout her core, and Tara had to act lest the sensation cause her to faint. She dived for the two embroiled combatants, crash-tackling into Mallel, which dragged Cronetta along with them, and they tumbled over the edge of the ridge.

It was a strange sensation—Tara realised—diving over a cliff, yet feeling as if she had started falling upwards. She did not realise it, but Votly would have explained that the little makeshift gondola they had used had enough relative gravity on it to keep them *mostly* grounded. But as they dived over it, on the far side from the approaching port, the port's mass and the gondola's mass added to one another, so instead of falling *down*, Tara and her company fell *inwards*.

They dragged and scraped to a halt on the far side of the makeshift gondola. Tara stumbled up and jammed her elbow into Cronetta's gut before she could react and then she dived over Mallel, covering him from the coming catastrophe.

In the final moment before impact, Cronetta grabbed for Tara, gripping one of the bandoliers of smoke bombs that lined her coat. With quick reflexes Tara slashed the fixture from her coat, and Cronetta tumbled away, carrying the belt of bombs along with her.

The rock smashed into the abandoned port with a thunderous crack, dipping into the ashen surface of the little world before physics realised it had a job to do involving equal and opposite reactions. The dust and debris from the collision expelled outwards in a slow-motion blast wave of dust, ice, and bits of old building.

There were larger chunks of rock in this blooming explosion, drifting further out into the gravity reefs in a chaotic spin.

Upon one of these Tara found herself gripping the stony surface while holding onto Mallel with all of her strength.

Mallel blinked away dust and debris from his eyes. Tara tried to stifle the sensation of ringing in her ears. The titanic thunderclap from the collision was now followed by a rolling thunder that was slowly dissipating from deafening to painfully loud.

"What in the Three Perversities?" Tara started, but stopped as Mallel pushed her from him and grabbed at his sword.

"Where is the bounty hunter?" he barked.

Tara's senses forced their way back into her awareness as the reality of the danger closed in. If they survived the impact, then so could Cronetta.

Mallel pulled a telescopic eyepiece from his coat and scanned the reefs. "There's something else out there."

"Where?" Tara's gaze darted throughout the expelled chaos. "I can't see it or Cronetta."

"It's ... it's two Slithmet, and behind them there is a gondola full of unsavoury-looking characters." Mallel's voice went hard. "We must rally our resolve, Tara. This battle is going to be tough."

"Tara Night!" a hissing voice boomed.

Tara snapped around to view the approaching enemy. The half-snake, half-humanoid form of Slithmet—metallic, rock-like sirens with a vicious torso of long limbs and talons, a fanged maw, and glowing red eyes—tore towards them through the ether. They swam upon self-induced electromagnetic currents in much the same way that the Beast propelled itself through the void.

"My cogrusted name is Star!" Tara yelled, and without a moment's hesitation, she pushed from the little meteor she was clinging to and leaped out into the space between her and the Slithmet.

Mallel cried out for some form of restraint, but Tara had already launched from his grasp. The ferocity surprised even her, and the benefit of that was that it surprised the Slithmet as well.

The first one scrambled mid-flight, its coiling tail whipping around to propel itself in the other direction. But its momentum was too much, and instead of gracefully evading Tara's trajectory—like she knew it could have if it wasn't surprised—it collided into her in a mess of tail and limbs with a yelp.

The force from the harder, more massive creature impacting on her was enough to knock the wind from her lungs. But she was accustomed to pain, and she was ready for it.

In the flying brawl she kneed the thing in the gut; cracking pains shot through her leg but also caused the Slithmet to grunt as she drew a throwing knife and jammed it in between the plates in its neck. There was a spark as metal slid against metallic stone and became lodged in the creature's exoskeleton. With a snarl it coiled around to snap its fangs over her head, but Mallel was there, having jumped himself from the little meteor, fly-kicking the Slithmet in the jaw with his hard boots.

The vicious maw cracked, and flakes of metallic stone flew from its faceplate. Tara crawled over its shoulder in the airborne brawl, pulling out another knife and jamming it in between the plates in the spine with another spark and yelp.

Mallel kept the fiend occupied with a frontal assault on its face while Tara clambered down the spine, jamming knives into each little kink she could find.

Until finally the three of them collided into the larger port asteroid—what was left of it at least—on the edge of a great drop-off into the void. Smoke and debris puffed up around them as the three sprawled across the crumbling grey soil. Tara coughed away the dust, the cloud around them clearing enough for her to make out the silhouette of the second Slithmet barrelling towards them from above.

"Cogrust." *We need to defeat this Slithmet before the next one gets to us.*

She scrambled onto her feet at the same time as Mallel did. He spat inky blue blood from his mouth as they squared up against the Slithmet rising in the dissipating dust cloud before them. Its insidious form a terrible imprint on the barren beauty of the gravity reefs behind it.

"You dare strike at me, little creatures. Do you not know we serve powers greater than you can comprehend?" it hissed.

"You mean the Rel?" Tara stepped forward, brandishing another knife.

Its red eyes flashed. "Indeed, it will deliver us from our suffering. All it wants in return is for your ruined corpses to be delivered to its scions. With the echoes of agony still present in your cold, lifeless eyes." It flashed its talons, and little black, sinewy tendrils burrowed between the cracks in its fingers.

"These things are suits," Tara hissed at Mallel. "There is something within it that is organic. Maybe not enough for a Rel scion to interfere with, hence why it has its own voice still … but maybe enough to infect something should it get close enough … The skull … that's why they want in on the skull …"

Mallel's eyes widened. "And if they get to it first, that's how they will be able to ensure the Beast devours our worlds."

"What are you two yapping about?" The Slithmet snapped its jaw.

"I was just thinking ..." Tara said. She nonchalantly stepped around the Slithmet. The tingling sensation rose within her, the Luck Symbioid urging some action that she desperately wanted to avoid. Her other symbioid—the Master Symbioid, the one capable of repelling the Rel scion—spiked, too, in the presence of the Rel, "... that this Rel has promised you a lot. And yet it can't even get to little old me?" She cocked her head, flicking the knives between her fingers.

The Slithmet coiled, ready to pounce.

Good.

The Luck Symbioid tingled.

Also good.

She tried to keep track of the other Slithmet barrelling towards them from above. It had halted, signalling the approaching gondola Mallel had pointed out as it drew closer, its tether skimming by the ruined port asteroid. *That's probably not so good.*

"I've defeated every Rel Scion I've come across so far," she said. "The thing you serve is a weak parasite of a being, and it chooses even weaker servants to do its bidding."

"Silence!" The Slithmet sprang forward, and Tara ducked forward at the same time as Mallel rushed its side.

Tara dodged the talon swipe and gripped the knife blade imbedded in its neck, her other hand reaching for one she had placed in its ribs. Mallel—as astute as ever—gripped the two blades she had imbedded in its spine. As the Slithmet spun to swipe back at them, Tara and Mallel wrenched their blade handles in opposite directions, snapping the exoskeleton plates and fracturing the Slithmet's armour along the kinks.

It screamed in terror as the exoskeleton crumbled around it, and it tumbled over the edge of the port's cliff. Its plates and armour and tail spindled out across the ether into obscurity.

The second Slithmet impacted on the crater behind them, and Tara and Mallel turned to face it.

"So you defeated my underling?" it hissed.

Tara's eyes flickered with recognition. "So you found another exoskeleton after all, Hoztic? We will still defeat you like we did your friend."

"Oh, I am not here to fight you." Hoztic cackled. "You see that?" He pointed to the other gondola skimming by the broken port. "That contains a war band of mine that is heading towards the skull. I am going to board it and leave you here; you will have a grand view from here when the Great One eats your puny worlds."

"Then why stop here at all?" Tara asked. "Perhaps the Rel has really husked your brain to make you do something so stupid as to risk yourself."

Hoztic sniggered. "Oh, if only you knew how much the Rel hated you. It did say you would tell me anything to convince me it is evil. Anything to save your kind ... which," he paused, "which I understand. But I would do anything to save mine. I am really, truly sorry." His eyes flashed crimson. "Just not sorry enough. The other reason I dropped in here was to say you're missing your belt of bombs, dear Tara ..."

Tara felt for her missing bandolier of smoke and incendiary bombs. "So?" she asked, pulling out another throwing knife. "I don't need those to kill you."

"But I need them, to help me break into the inner sanctum of the skull." Hoztic looked around. "Cronetta, where are you?"

A coughing and spluttering form emerged from one of the cratered buildings and ambled up to Hoztic; in one arm she held the belt of bombs.

"You see, Tara," Hoztic continued, "Cronetta was guiding us towards you with a flashing beacon of light. And with it, we had a discussion. We can use your bombs, we realised. Especially after that little display with the gas geysers. And now, you're marooned on this little rock."

The gondola drew closer, and a raucous jeering from the warriors on board washed over the four people standing by the port's cliff.

"Until next time, little bounty hunter." Cronetta whipped her rope dart out towards the gondola while Hoztic held onto her. With a grunt, the rope dart struck the gondola as it streamed by, and the two were yanked from the world, leaving Tara and Mallel in their wake.

"No!" Tara sped after them and made to dive off the cliff after the gondola, but was crash-tackled into the ground by Mallel.

"It's too far, Tara," he said as she struggled to throw him off her. "Tara, you'll die out there. We'll find another way."

"No!" was all Tara could scream as Hoztic's gondola grew distant in the reefs, heading towards the massive form of the Beast. "We can't let him win!"

"Tara." Mallel held her closer, stifling her cries, which turned to sobs. "We'll find another way. Have faith."

The symbioid flared. Tara shot up out of Mallel's embrace and looked at a hanging rock that listed precariously over the edge of the gravity reefs. They came this far on what was essentially a rocky raft to begin with. Why not a smaller one?

"Tara," Mallel said warily. "What are you going to do?"

Tara turned to face him. "I'm going after them. You can stay here or come with me."

She turned from Mallel and sprinted for the listing rock. She leaped onto it, and it cracked, leaning further out over the void. Tara felt her gut drop. But the rock held. Until Mallel charged up behind her, landing on the rock, which split and tumbled into the ether after the enemy gondola.

CHAPTER 15

Snipes

He fell through chaos.

It was a mad-dash tumble down rapids of viscous sludge that smelled of … well … Snipes knew he had left the stomach but refused to realise that meant he was now churning through the intestines … and that sludge around him was now … well … crap.

Luckily he didn't have to spend too much time thinking about it. Chunks of the planetoid the Beast had consumed still protruded from the near vertical current, and Snipes was bashed, struck, and concussed the whole way through the twisting, cave-like conduit.

The keening wail of the Infyrra followed behind him, muted as it sloshed against the same undigested rock that had knocked Snipes about.

He was safe from it for now; all he had to do was survive the falling mayhem.

After a time, Snipes woke—not realising he had passed out—and coughed and spluttered. He was wasted along a sinewy shore among soft mounds of drying soil.

Don't think about it.

He pulled himself to his feet, glad to know he couldn't smell what he stood in. He patted down his nose to find it wasn't broken—though his body felt like cracked glass—and he was also surprised to find he wasn't drenched, but relatively dry.

He scanned the cavernous walls, which shifted with feelers and tubes that sucked the moisture from the very air with a slurping sound. The ground shifted slightly, the soil travelling slowly along the cavern floor in a rhythmic motion that made Snipes queasy.

"Right," Snipes wheezed, "questions for later."

Around the bend in the cavern was a throbbing opening. It yawned open and closed by contracting muscles that pumped sections of the soil further along the cavern ahead of him. As the opening widened, a light flashed, followed by the sound of crashing metal, the titanic hiss of a prism cannon, and a familiar swear word.

"Shards!" The curse travelled throughout the cavern before it was drowned out by the sounds of conflict yet again. Yet a small echo of it buzzed in the earpiece Flayr had given Snipes earlier.

"The Light Wizards!" Snipes perked up and shuffled down the cavern, looking over his shoulder to check for the pursuing Infyrra—it was not there.

He rounded the bend and ducked through to the next cavern as the contracting muscles opened it again. He stopped mid-stride—or mid-stumble as he tried to keep his balance over the shifting soils—and gasped in wonder.

It was ... incredible.

The chrome hull of the *Motebeam* was imbedded in the side of a gelatinous ridge across the great cavernous space. It looked much the same way as when Snipes first found it wrecked upon the Baul Islands back on his world. Now it was under siege yet again. Not from a motley band of angry locals, but from towering guardians of sinew and spine. These creatures stood tall, much like the statue corpse he had found in the acid swamps of the stomach. Yet while living, these beings were bound in muscle and tendrils, and they assailed the ship with huge blows that dented the hull.

Every so often, a prism cannon would fire, and one of the guardians—the Custanguin—would falter back with a keening wail, only to be replaced by another.

"Come on, you bastards! I'll shatter you all into shards!" A Prismath engineer was atop one of the inactive cannons, flanked by shooters. One was a marine and one a rifleman.

Squabbles don't mean much in the face of an external threat, Snipes realised. "Ah, Motebeam?" He tapped the strange little communication device in his ear.

The marine stationed by the engineer perked up, scanning the bowels of the Beast after firing a beam into the head of an approaching Custanguin. It groaned and took a ground-rattling step back.

"Is that one of the Stemcogs?" the marine asked.

"Yeah, this is Snipes." A keening roar echoed behind Snipes. He dashed forward across the open space of the cavern. Behind him, the Infyrra rounded the corner and spilled into the space, rolling after him. "Ah, I'm under attack."

"Shocking news, you scattered moron!" the rifleman barked. "We all are!"

"And whose fault was that?" the engineer retorted over the radio.

"Guys!" Snipes snapped as he bolted forward. He realised that the Custanguin had paused their assault and turned on him ... or ... more accurately, on the Infyrra pursuing him. "Can we kill each other *after* we survive this?"

"Sure thing, Snipes." Another marine was atop a gun deck on the *Motebeam* and turned the barrels of their prism guns on the blob surging behind Snipes. He opened fire and seared the Infyrra back before it lashed a tendril around his leg. "You better get moving; you're about to be caught up in a brawl."

"Roger that!"

Snipes dashed forward, and the titanic Custanguin charged towards him, their thundering steps shaking the bowels and rattling the ground as Snipes tried to step between their paths. The quaking rattled up his bones and sent tremors across his ribs as he tried to keep his footing, as he tried not to let the anxiety of unsteady ground overwhelm him.

And then, the squadron of Custanguin were past him, smashing into the gelatinous pink monster that had ravaged the innards of the Beast and killed their comrades. Snipes couldn't help but turn and witness the absolute insanity of it all.

The hard-edged figures of the guardians lashed into a tidal wave of pink anguish. The moaning and wailing of the contest rippled throughout the space as the Infyrra slowly pulled the Custanguin into its absorbing embrace, and their thrashing forms sunk into it with slowing movements.

"They won't last long," Snipes realised, remembering the desiccated corpse of the Custanguin in the acid swamps. "It'll dissolve their sinew in a matter of minutes."

"Well, it's given us time to work on the cannons," the engineer said. "Get yourself on board, Stemcog, NOW!"

Snipes did not need to be told twice. He tore his eyes away from the insane titanic war being raged within the lower bowels of the Beast and sprinted for the *Motebeam*. A gun deck extended from the upper hull with two shooters unspooling a harness and lowering it down into the squishy marsh. The area around the *Motebeam* was all torn up and swamp-like after the assault from the Custanguin. Snipes squelched into the battleground, grinding his teeth as his feet sank into the damp soil, and hit the swaying harness at a run.

As he struggled to hang on, dozens of repair crews were pouring out of other service hatches. They worked to clear the damaged gunports so the main cannons could be brought through.

"He's got a grip!" a Marine called from above.

With a whirring mechanical strain, the harness yanked Snipes from the muddy soil with a plopping sound, and he spun chaotically as he ascended to the gun deck.

"You good there, sniper?" A marine grabbed Snipes's coat with a powerful hand and pulled him over the railing onto the gun deck.

Snipes rolled over and retched, but he hadn't eaten in days, it felt like, and nothing came out.

He pushed himself up and said resolutely, "It's Snipes." He glanced at the rolling, tidal battle as the last of the Custanguin were pulled into the ebbing flow of the Infyrra's folds. "Now what's the situation with the *Motebeam*?"

Snipes was ushered into the depths of the ship, trotting through beam-seared corridors, blue-blood-spattered floors, and the wrecked form of a Slithmet. The fighting during the attempted coup had been intense, but the few remaining squadrons of marines and riflemen both seemed to be more focused on the threat outside the ship than on the ones within, for the moment.

"That pink thing is rallying to storm the *Motebeam*," a voice said over the loudspeakers. "It's taking its time, though; it seems to be struggling to digest those guardians that were attacking us."

"What's the time frame?" the marine escorting Snipes to the bridge asked over his comms device.

The reply came over the loudspeaker. "About five minutes, but who knows?"

"Will that be enough time?" Snipes asked the marine as they entered the battle-scarred bridge. There was a haphazard group of technicians and soldiers trying their best to coordinate things in the ruined room. None of them were command crew, Snipes realised. The command crew were the tip of the spear that slammed into the Beast's skull; the people here were doing their best but were out of their depth.

"Will it?" the marine asked one of the gun crew who was desperately trying to get a console to work by bashing the top of it.

"This whole system is in shards," the crewman spat. "We can get the cannons out individually, but we can't coordinate fire. We'll have to fire sporadically."

A hum tore through the ship as one of the cannons did just that. "Incoming!" a panicked voice said over the speakers.

Snipes rushed to the observation screen and watched as the gelatinous mass of the Infyrra swarmed towards the *Motebeam*, fired on by stray white-and-red beams from the cannons.

"The cannon fire!" someone on the bridge bellowed. "It's pushing it back!"

The Infyrra slinked and shrivelled under the cannon fire, searing beams burning away its putrid flesh and feelers as it shuddered and recoiled.

A cheer went up around the bridge.

It retreated to the edge of the cavern where the contracting muscles still pumped more of the drying soil into the space.

"Fire on that orifice!" Snipes ordered.

The crewman hurriedly spoke into his earpiece, and some of the cannons targeted the orifice. The whole Beast rumbled in pain as the orifice closed over, and the Infyrra pressed up against the fleshy wall ... trapped.

"It can't go anywhere!" the marine cheered. "Keep firing!"

Snipes watched with trepidation as the Infyrra withered under fire, torn apart and sizzled to pieces. He allowed himself to sigh with relief as the smoke from burning organic matter rose from it. "The people of these parts will be glad to be rid of that thing." He laughed.

"New contacts emerging!" another lookout cried.

Snipes leaned forward, peering into the murk with horror as angular shapes jutted out of the quivering Infyrra's body.

"It's the guardians!" the marine said. "They're still alive!"

"No." A shiver travelled down Snipes's spine. "They're not alive."

Their sinew was now stripped from them, and only their carapaces remained, like the one he found in the acid swamps of the stomach. Only now the pink tendril feelers of the Infyrra were weaving their way into their joints and armour.

The pink blob dwindled as it poured itself into the group of Custanguin corpses, connected by stray feelers that ended in a globular node by the wall at the end of the cavern.

"Our cannons couldn't stop those things!" the marine cursed. "And they're covering the pink thing; we can't get a clear shot at it!"

"The Infyrra will use them to rip open our hull," Snipes realised. "Then it will pour itself in here and consume us all."

"What do we do?" a frantic technician asked.

Snipes clenched his eyes shut, remembering his blunderbuss buried deep within the creature's innards, loaded with his flechette rounds. "If I can get to my gun, I can disrupt it. I'll cut the tendrils from the Custanguin, and then you can roast it with the cannons."

"Where is your gun?" a rifleman asked.

Snipes gritted his teeth. "I'm going to need one of your void suits."

* * *

Snipes found himself standing on the lowered cargo ramp of the *Motebeam*. The strange fleshy and skeletal insides of the Beast's innards were laid out before him, covered in soil—he refused to think of it as anything else. The army of zombiefied Custanguin charged the *Motebeam*, barely kept at bay by the cannons.

Snipes stepped into the churning, muddy surface once more. He looked through his visor, past the rank of Custanguin, to the blobby pink node that controlled them.

"Keep those guardians occupied," Snipes said over the comms. "I just need time."

"You'll get it," a marine replied. "Good luck, sniper."

Snipes rolled his eyes and dashed down the ramp. He moved around the raging battlefield, feet plopping into the half-drying, half-marshy ground with sickening squelches. The Custanguin were too occupied to notice him as they weathered unceasing cannon fire. Each blaze of light hummed against their metallic exoskeletons, the dazzling display outshining the strobing luminosity that channelled constantly down the Beast's insides.

It took a few minutes of panicked scrambling over sinew and strange, spongy appendages to get around their flank before Snipes had a straight shot to the node. It trembled, and some of the feelers on its outsides bent like stems in the breeze, pointing towards him.

"Cogrust!"

Snipes looked over his shoulder as one of the lumbering Custanguin turned from its assault on the *Motebeam* and rounded on him. It *galloped* towards him, every gigantic step bringing it closer. Snipes had only one place to go.

He steeled himself and charged for the node. The rumbling of the approaching defender grew more violent with each step. Snipes sprinted as hard as he could in the bulky suit through the marshy ground, even as the shadow of the Custanguin engulfed him, even as its mighty hand reached out to squash him ...

Snipes slammed into the flesh of the seared Infyrra node.

It engulfed him with a plop, and Snipes found himself immersed in the horrid, hellish insides of the dissolving monster. Goo and feelers both enshrouded him in a caustic embrace, dissolving the suit's fittings and cracking the glass of his visor. But Snipes soldiered on.

He waded through the horrid insides, ignoring the blaring warnings that his suit assailed him with, warning him of the failing integrity of the materials. In that churning hell, Snipes closed his eyes and breathed. The ground may not have been solid beneath his feet, but he did not need it to be to complete his task.

He was taken back to that fateful day when the ground gave way beneath him, alerting the group of child thugs to his presence, forcing him to kill them before they killed him and Thomas. The guilt and sorrow and anxiety swirled around him like the caustic substances that surrounded him now.

"I will atone!" he screamed into the maelstrom.

He refused to buckle, even as the acids wormed their way through his suit and assailed his skin, scalding, burning. He did not give in even as the feelers of the Infyrra tripped his feet and caused him to stumble. He still soldiered on. He was a Hired Hero, and he would complete his mission.

"I will atone!" He lashed out, pulling down a feeler that tried to block his path, and he found his objective.

His modified blunderbuss lay ensnared in tendrils. It was treated with coated alloys, so it was marred but currently unharmed by the Infyrra's best efforts. The clip had been ejected, the flechette rounds missing, but that did not matter. He had more.

He grasped his weapon as he pulled the last of his flechette rounds from the webbing strapped around his waist. He slammed the new clip into the chamber as the feelers strangled him and as the acids burned at the parts of his skin that were now exposed.

Tara's words came to his mind as he raised the blunderbuss to fire.

"I will atone. Even if the world crumbles around me, I am unshakable!" He squeezed the trigger.

The flechette round exploded from the barrel, fracturing in a hail of fire and metal, and spreading out in a cone of burning, razor-sharp shrapnel. The vibrations rippled out from the Infyrra's body as the shot tore through sinew and goop and exploded out the outer layer. The Infyrra shrieked and receded, and Snipes charged through the rippling opening. He burst out of the cancerous innards as the Infyrra ripped its controlling feelers from the dead Custanguin.

They froze and crumbled in their assault on the *Motebeam* as Snipes charged into the open. He racked the bolt on his gun, loading another flechette round into his blunderbuss, and turned on his foe. But it had lunged towards him in moaning fury; it slapped the gun from his hands and broke it with force against the leg of a Custanguin; then it charged towards him.

Snipes turned and ran. "Fire, fire, fire!" he cried.

The beams of the *Motebeam* lanced over his shoulder, searing the Infyrra as it pursued him around the cover of the guardians. Light and explosions and alien screaming followed in his wake as Snipes ran and ducked and jumped and slid towards the ship.

"We can't get a clear shot! It's too small now; it abandoned its mass in the guardians!" a panicked voice said over the comms.

Snipes made it to the cargo ramp, and it closed behind him as the cancerous blob smashed into the hull, rocking the ship with the force of it.

"Sniper!" The voice was over the loudspeakers. "It's on the hull, forcing its way into the hatches and cracks. Our cannons can't shoot it!"

"Cogrust!" Snipes slammed his fists against the chrome flooring as the ship lurched.

"It's getting inside!"

Snipes's mind raced. "We're at the end of the Beast's digestive tract," he said to himself.

"What?" The reply came from the crewman on the bridge.

Snipes didn't realise he was still speaking into the radio. "What is the *Motebeam* lodged in?" he asked, raising his eyes to look at the ceiling of the cargo hold as it lurched and rumbled.

"We're in some kind of orifice!"

"Fire on the walls," Snipes ordered.

"WHAT?"

The hull around the cargo bay was lit by strafing sparks and horrible metal screeching as the Infyrra assailed it with corrosive feelers and acids.

"Fire now before the Infyrra breaks the hull; fire everything on the walls now!"

"Do it!" a marine bellowed over the comms. "All cannon crew, swivel guns and fire on the wall!"

The whole ship hummed as every cannon available charged and opened fire on the walls of the Beast. The Beast rumbled in agony again, and the whole ship lurched more violently this time. Snipes was thrown into the air as the ship dropped—the orifice around them recoiling in reflex to the sudden pain—and Snipes slammed into the high ceiling of the cargo hold only to slam back down into the floor.

The ship screeched as if the walls were being grated against on all sides. With a titanic whoosh of air, the *Motebeam* lurched again, this time slamming Snipes into the side wall. The wind was knocked from him. The last vestiges of the void suit's casings broke around him, and he was sure he had internal injuries.

"What happened?" he wheezed.

"We've been expelled!" An engineer rushed up to support him. The Prismath looked like he had a broken nose but was otherwise unhurt.

"What?" Snipes groaned.

"We shot out of the Beast's anus!" the engineer shouted in anxious glee.

"Huh?" Snipes knew that was his plan, but he still couldn't quite believe it.

"Its anus! We just got sha ..."

A screen flicked to life on the wall as another injured engineer brought up the outside image. The view was strange. They were drifting away from the underside of the Beast as the Infyrra detached itself from the hull. Its feelers reached for the Beast's extremities before it pulled too far away, before it reached the vacuum.

"Gun crews," Snipes croaked, but then his voice hardened. "Incinerate it!"

"Roger that!"

The Infyrra was lit up by dozens of red beams as the cannons targeted it, and then with muted hums as the cannons charged, the red was replaced by white. The ship's cannons hummed and boomed as they discharged their payload. Each beam was like a lance of fire that dismembered the Infyrra to ribbons and then incinerated those into oblivion.

"It's done." Snipes all but collapsed. "It's dead."

He was vaguely aware of hitting the floor as crew members rushed in to aid him.

Votly

It was a strange sort of battle—Votly knew that even with her meagre experience fighting in the field. Prism marines and riflemen traded potshots from afar while their newly acquired allies—the Ekelts and the Culs—advanced on each other in a vicious brawl of bludgeoning and slicing.

As far as things went, the battle was pretty even. The Culs and riflemen were more numerous, putting the Ekelts and marines at the disadvantage in terms of overwhelming power. But the riflemen weren't good shots, not as good as the marines at least, and when an Ekelt got shot, it wasn't necessarily an incapacitating blow.

Conversely, the marines gunned down a good swathe of the Culs as they surged forward. Their calloused hides may have been tough, but they weren't as beam-proof as the Ekelts' exoskeletons.

The magnetic atmosphere reeked of burned flesh while the splaying lights of the prism beams danced about the ghastly landscape. The screams of battle echoed across the spires of the Beast's spine.

Votly was keeping on top of things as best she could. The battle did not tip this way or that for a good while, and she predicted it would remain this way for the foreseeable future. That was until the Culs or the Ekelts would break through each other and engage either the marines or riflemen. The fear of this had settled into a constant frustration, as every time she tried to get her marines to inch closer, they were kept at bay. And every time the Beast's body swayed through the ether, she could see two growing dots of light across the unfathomable distance, her world and Tara's.

Something had to give; she just wasn't expecting what happened next.

The battlefield was rocked by an earthquake ... or, more accurately, a Beast quake.

Votly hadn't noticed it at first.

Her Light Gauntlet lit up with a signal from the *Motebeam*, and she gazed down at it in wonder as the image of the ship appeared down the tail end of the Beast.

The first she knew of the quake was when Curla cried out and tumbled from cover, followed by a commiserating cry from all of the other combatants as they were lifted from their feet and slammed down again.

Votly was unceremoniously deposited into a ditch with Curla.

The pangs of pain scrubbed the image of the holographic *Motebeam* from her mind, as sharp edges and hard impacts are wont to do.

"Shards!" She wasn't *usually* one to swear.

Befuddled, she shakily pulled herself out of the ditch while struggling to draw a breath into her winded body. The breath came as a whimper, and then it morphed into an uneven sob. The pain flooded out of her eyeballs in the form of an emotion unbefitting the current commander of the deadliest fighters in the sun well.

"I can't do this!" she sobbed.

"Techie," Curla wheezed as she pulled herself out from rubble, "what in the shattered calamity just happened?"

"I don't know!" Votly cried, throwing her hands up.

Curla was regathering her wits, dragging herself towards Votly to place her hand over her mouth. "Shh! We got thrown around a bit there; there's no telling where the enemy is."

Votly wanted to shout, to scream that she didn't care. She had been boarded, jettisoned over the back of a war-torn space leviathan, and then watched Balt die from fire that should have been friendly.

Those bastards! She gritted her teeth. All of a sudden, she didn't care about the horrid time she had been through. Not as if she was ready to give up, or quit, or cry again. Instead, she didn't care that the enemy was close, or that the *Motebeam* might have just been jettisoned out of the Beast's arse into the cosmos, and that they were likely marooned on the back of this inhospitable being.

She just wanted more of those traitorous riflemen to pay.

A Cul pulled itself over the edge of the ditch they had been thrown into.

Maybe I won't even get the chance to do that much. Votly almost laughed as her breath returned, and Curla drew her hand away from her mouth to find a weapon.

"King dead," it said in a deep voice with a quivering lip.

"Huh?" Curla froze mid-draw, realising her holster was empty anyway, but the thing seemed too dumb to realise, so why let it know?

"King dead … need your king to decide." It cocked its head, like it was saying something completely reasonable under the circumstances.

"Your leader is dead?" Votly ventured.

It nodded its head enthusiastically; the quivering lip seemed to be a biological feature rather than an emotion.

"And you want us to decide what to do about it?" Curla gaped.

It shook its head then pointed at Votly. "Your king," it jutted its thumb over its shoulder, "your other king … you decide … come now." It reached in and grabbed them both with powerful limbs, dragging them out of the ditch and into the wider spine of the Beast.

As far as damage from the quake, there wasn't any. The Beast still undulated throughout the cosmos—a little speedier actually, Votly noticed in despair—and the only real damage was done to the combatants on the field. Votly gasped as she found the king Ekelt shattered and smeared across the ground.

"And your king?" Votly asked.

The Cul pointed up. Votly followed his gesture and almost screamed. Dozens of writhing figures were somersaulting throughout the night sky *away* from the Beast. The movement that had caused the quake must have sent them flying so far as to escape the gravitational pull the Beast commanded.

"How far does the atmosphere go?" Curla asked aloud.

"Not far enough." Votly scanned the figures with her Light Gauntlet. "We've taken casualties too."

"I don't want to think about it," Curla spat. "I want to ram my boot down their throat, though!" Curla found some riflemen being corralled by a group of Ekelts and stalked forward, only to be stopped by the Cul who had dragged them from the ditch.

"Not you, king," the Cul said. "Our king's dead; you decide."

"Decide what?" Curla snapped.

"They want us to decide who will lead." The voice was cocky and cold, and Votly recognised it instantly: Keihn.

"You bastard!" Votly bit her lip, rounding on the pompous corporal whose arm was in a filthy sling. "You." She stepped forward. "Selfish. Bastard!" She reared her hand, but it was caught by the Cul.

"Not here, arena," it said.

"Huh?"

"They want the remaining kings to solve this issue, now that theirs are dead," Keihn sneered.

"And how did you become king of the riflemen?" Curla hissed.

Keihn shrugged, grimacing as his wounded shoulder moved. "I'm the one who convinced the Cul king you lot were here to steal their water. And now, sweet little Votly," his leering gaze turned towards her, "I get to kill you."

"What do you mean?" Curla said as Votly shrunk back.

"The dispute will be solved by single combat," Keihn's eyes never left Votly, "between you and me."

* * *

What happened next was hard to describe.

There was a stunned silence from the marines who were being corralled into the space, then an all-out eruption as marine and rifleman both rose up in abject anger—Votly would later ponder on how even the riflemen came to her defence.

The Ekelts and Culs actively supported *each other* as they bludgeoned back the two warring Prismath parties, until one Cul's agitated voice broke out over the bedlam.

"All kings but you two are dead. I don't know why this is a problem, but it is, so we will bind you all and take you to the place of reckoning!"

The Ekelts and Culs wordlessly worked together. They bound the hands of the Prismath factions and led them laterally across the spine of the Beast, moving down its side where one of its titanic fins swam through the ether. It was a trek that took half the day, or half of what felt like a day at least. Votly kept gazing skullwards to where her home world grew distressingly larger. They didn't have time for this.

They seemed to be heading for the "armpit," where the fin met the rest of the body. Their path took them deep into what could only be described as a ravine that was rich with giant fungi plants and other creatures of varying appearance and apparent sentience. The air grew heavy, hot, and damp.

More moisture oozed from this place as the Beast swam. It was a sweat gland.

Curla was lockstep with Votly, their hands bound behind their backs as they were force-marched. The Ekelts flanked one side, the Culs the other.

"They're almost friendly towards each other now," Votly wondered on their march, gazing between the two alien species.

"Don't you see what that means?" Curla hissed, and rolled her eyes when Votly gave her a look. "It means that when Keihn kills you, he'll have the Culs, the Ekelt, and the riflemen following his orders."

"When he kills me." Votly bit down on the bile rising in her throat. "What am I going to do?"

"What indeed." Curla bit her lip. "What indeed ..."

Votly gazed at the closest Ekelt to her. "Will we get weapons?"

It rounded on her, and one of its eye sockets clicked wider. "Only what you wear."

"Shards," Curla hissed again. "Keihn has an energy knife and a prism pistol under those robes of his. What do you have?"

Votly flexed her arm, the gauntlet around her wrist straining. "I'll have enough." She turned back to the Ekelt. "And where are we going to have this duel?"

"At the great reservoir, the place where our kings first took issue with one another during the great drought." The Ekelt turned forward. "Now silence yourself, potential king. We are approaching."

They crested another craggy piece of the Beast's exoskeleton with the fin swaying above them like a great tower about to topple over. It blotted out swathes of stars and enshrouded the eclectic band in shadow. And that's when they saw it—a pulsating cloud of indigo blue deeper in the ravine—the pit— it emanated from the depths.

"We're going straight to the deepest point of the pit," Votly realised.

She looked over her shoulder, where Keihn was leering. She remembered the threats he had made against her on the *Motebeam*. He was going to enjoy this. Votly did her best to glare back. She would not let him have his victory.

The air grew heavier as they trudged into the hallowed space; every rumbling undulation of the Beast was louder here. It was like a great rolling thunder that set you on edge. The thick atmosphere clung to their skin, and the metallic fittings of their clothes, harnesses, armour, and weapons were pulled in odd directions as the magnetic currents pirouetted and swirled about the deepening space. The magnetic thrum of the Beast's electromagnetic propulsion coursed every time it took a stroke through the space between stars.

Instead of growing dimmer as they descended, it grew paler.

They passed by little villages, huts, and caverns that were carved into the exoskeletal structure where the different species of inhabitants scurried out of sight and watched their passage from the shadows.

Then they finally reached their destination. It was an arena.

The space was cragged and marred by stones and ridges with gouges, signs from battles past. It was lined with a tiered series of ridges that would allow for hundreds of spectators.

The Culs and the Ekelts herded the Prismath into the seating areas around the arena, while one large Cul took Votly and Keihn by their bonds and guided them into the centre.

The Cul turned to them, pulled out a jagged knife, and cut their bonds. Then it shoved them away from each other.

The Cul then turned to the assembled crowd.

Votly's breath was in her throat; she tried not to look at Keihn's sinister stare. The arena seating was being filled by the other people they had passed on their way here. There were little gremlin creatures, strange fungus things, and other Culs and Ekelts who wore different garb than that of their warriors. There was a murmur of excitement from the gathering species, a tribal grunt from the Culs, and a strange, keening erupting from the Ekelts as they rubbed their scythes together.

"When The Great One ..." the Cul boomed, and the growing hum hushed in an instant, "... swam away from the fertile nebulas, into the deep, into the fringes of the stars, our ways of life were brutalised!"

There was a chattering of agreement.

"He no longer produced enough nectar to sustain our tribes, he grew sickly and weak, and our people grew sick with him. None were fit to lead; we were directionless. Then the enemies came, great growths of disease from within his scales, slithering enemies from fresh worlds that were trawled in his wake. But the Custanguin fought off the diseases, and we routed the mighty Slithmet, and new kings emerged. So we fought over this sacred font, for control. Our kings are now dead! But two new ones have emerged. They will fight here, and we will be the judges."

The Cul turned to Votly and Keihn, nodded, and shuffled out of the arena.

Votly gazed up at her marines, who watched helplessly, still bound on the upper tiers. The riflemen, too, watched on with morbid fascination. She looked back to Keihn.

"I bet you wish your Stemcog friend was here," he spat. "Maybe she would save you, or maybe not; maybe she would burn you to death like poor Sreckle."

"When she met us," Votly gritted her teeth, "she was trying to stop us from destroying another innocent city. Doesn't that keep you up at night, Keihn? What we did to those people?"

"That was Mallel, not me!" Keihn lunged forward and slapped Votly, who gasped and fell back as the onlookers cheered, as the marines cursed and pulled against their bonds, and as the riflemen watched silently. "I'm just a corporal! I was dragged along on this journey. I had no say in the matter … I had no choice!" Keihn pressed the attack, stamping at Votly's prone form as she scrambled back between rocks and nooks and crannies which tripped Keihn up in his anger.

"No, you had no choice!" Votly kicked out at him with her boots as he stumbled. She struck his jaw when he stooped low, and his head snapped back. "But you willingly brought the enemy onto our ship!" Her timidness dissolved with her anger … no, not anger … *fury*, righteous, bloody fury. She pounced on him and scratched at his eyes and kicked and kneed at his crotch. "You made the choice to take up arms against your own people! You killed marines, you got your own riflemen killed, and you left Bromean to get executed by that monster! And you held me hostage, all so that the enemy could use our home as a battering ram to get into this Beast's skull! I hate you! I hate you! Scrond would be ashamed to call you one of his crew!"

Keihn grabbed her fist with a snarl. He winced as he used his bad arm, but he was still strong enough to hold her. "If Bromean died it's because you killed him!" He punched upwards, smacking Votly's nose.

Her vision went white as a sickening crack exploded in her eardrums, and she rocked back onto her arse.

"Scrond is dead, the last Prismatist," Keihn said. Votly blinked away the pain and wiped her face, only for gushing blue blood to cling to her hands. "Do you really think he would have brought those Stemcogs into the fold if he had no other choice?"

"Yes, I knew what he would have done. I knew him better than you, Keihn. He was training me to be a Prismatist." Votly tried to get up but stumbled back. She was no warrior; she was spent.

"Well, you're no fighter, you're no leader, and you're definitely no Prismatist!" Keihn spat, drawing his pistol from under his coat and aiming it at Votly. "You're just a useless techie!"

The words cut through Votly like a blade, the same ones she had said to Tara upon the hull of the *Motebeam*.

Tara. Votly wondered what Tara would do in this situation.

Tara, Votly realised, would already have won this fight. But failing that, she would have told Votly exactly what she needed to hear ... she already had.

Votly fiddled with her Light Gauntlet as Keihn marched over to execute her at point-blank range. "You're right," she hissed, "I'm no Prismatist."

Keihn laughed and pulled the trigger.

"I'm a Light Wizard!" Votly cried.

She raised her gauntlet as Keihn's beam fired. It struck the lens Votly had flipped in place, and she used the principles of Wave-Form that Scrond had taught her to do what Tara would call "magic." The light refracted within the main lens and then channelled through a series of smaller magnifying devices. It reinforced upon itself in waves and waves of humming, brilliant fury, until the lens could not handle the might of the reverberating energy.

It exploded outwards in a powerful beam of light.

The light nearly blinded her. The recoil nearly tore her arm out of her socket, but she held her aim firm. The beam of power ripped a hole in Keihn's chest and exploded out the other side; he didn't even have time to scream as he was pulled back by the trailing force and smashed into the far wall of the arena.

Votly heaved, panicked and out of breath, blinking away the brightness that nearly blinded her, and as the cheering erupted from the spectators—muted by the ringing in her ears—she collapsed.

Thundering footsteps leaped from the tiered ridges and trundled over to her. Huge hands and spindly appendages hauled her unwillingly to her feet as Votly threw up and was turned to face the roaring crowds. The riflemen were stunned silent; the marines were shaking themselves out of their own bewilderment and starting to scream wildly.

Curla was yanking at her bonds with a savagery to break free and hop down to Votly.

"Let the grey cloaks free," Votly croaked.

She hoped that these creatures could discern colour like her kind could.

One of the Ekelts cried out a rattling bark, and the bonds of the marines were cut. As soon as they were free, they were clambering or jumping down to shoo away the Culs and Ekelts and rushing to help Votly stand.

"You did it!" Curla exclaimed, taking Votly's face in her hands and examining her broken nose. "How *did* you do it?"

"Wizardry." Votly smiled. "I still have work to do, back away." The words weren't forceful, but Curla jumped back despite herself, as did the other marines. Votly addressed the crowd. "You've been fighting over the nectar?" There was a hushed murmuring. "It shall all be divided ..." Votly caught herself from saying equally. The Culs and Ekelts, the fungi things, and those little gremlin creatures all probably had different levels of need for the stuff, "... equitably ... among the people until the plight is passed."

"It won't last, though," one of the Culs boomed. "The plight still rages within the Great One."

"We're going to stop it!" Votly cried. "I want every warrior among you to follow me and my people out of this ..." she nearly said pit, "... font, and towards the skull. I will turn this Beast around to feast on the nebulas once more."

There was a hushed stillness from the crowd, and then a Cul stepped forward. "KING!"

The chant echoed throughout the strange assortment of creatures. "King! King! King!"

"What about them?" Curla gestured to the riflemen.

"Keep them bound," Votly said, "and bring them with us. We have an army now, but I fear we may not reach the skull to help Mallel and Tara in time."

"What can we do?" a breathless marine asked.

Votly looked down at her Light Gauntlet, sizzling and sputtering as it was, and then used it to try to raise her *Dustmote.*

CHAPTER 17

Tara Star

The passage of their little rocky raft was strange.

Tara clung to the edges while Mallel held her in place, and the impossible winds ruffled through their coats and hair as they fell for what felt like hours. Their slither of a vessel tumbled in an arch skullwards in the wake of Hoztic's gondola.

"Tara," Mallel said with a strained voice. His limbs were quivering from holding the two in place for so long, and his dark knuckles were tense and going white. "There." He shifted his weight and pulled out his looking glass, extending it with a whipping motion in one hand and pressing it to his eye to scan the landscape.

She braved the torrents and raised her head to see the great expanding land beneath them that was the Beast's neck at the base of its wide, impossible skull. It was a shimmering grey dome that emerged out of the spine and eventually tapered into the gaping maw of the star Beast. Its celestial eyes cratered into deep wells that gazed into the abyss and reflected the myriad of star stuff and nebula. Tara was aware of the golden glow emanating off the cracked skull plate which represented her native sun as they drew closer towards their worlds.

The worlds hung in the dark as pinpoint specks of light, growing at what felt like a glacial pace. But she knew they were travelling far faster than appearances would suggest, and that the Beast would close with their worlds soon enough should they fail to stop the Rel from influencing it.

She squinted and could just make out the pale green shape of her world's shattered moon. That was not a good sign.

"Where are they?" Tara said.

She did not have the telescopic eyepiece that Mallel gazed through.

"Do you see the cracks all down the skull? That must have been where the *Motebeam* struck it as Votly engaged the Wave-Form engine. The cracks are oozing some kind of blood. At the base of the skull there are titanic beings doing battle with a battalion of Slithmet and hordes of other creatures."

Tara squinted through the wind, and sure enough, Mallel was right. There were colossal things emerging from the cracks in the Beast's skull plate, creatures of skeletal rock and wiry sinew that fought against the harassing Slithmet. They fought savagely but to no avail. More war parties moved up to support the Rel's hapless servants.

She traced the fissure line of one of the skull's cracks to a point where a chunk of exoskeleton had been blown right off.

In the gap a phalanx of the skeletal giants fought a desperate last stand.

"Those giants must be those Custanguin things I heard about," Tara said. "They fight to protect the Beast and all the people who live on it from what I can gather. They must have been what repelled the Rel's initial invasion, and they've been limping on ever since. If the Slithmet get past them and inside the skull itself, if they can get a piece of the Rel directly into the brain stem, then it's all over."

"Then we need to get into the brain stem first, and kill this creature," Mallel said.

Tara sighed. "Captain ... people live on this thing. They rely on it for their lives the same as we do for our own worlds. If you kill this creature, you condemn untold thousands to their deaths."

"And yet again, Tara, what would you have me do?" Mallel sighed back. "Untold millions reside on our worlds. Would you have me weigh their lives against these relative few?"

Tara shut her eyes, remembering the town she had passed through when she was first marooned on the gravity reef world. Kids, couples, families, people just living their lives as best they could. She remembered the lights and neon signs of dozens of other similar towns shining across the dozens of other worlds here.

"Yes," Tara said, shifting to look at Mallel, her breath in her throat at his close presence. "If I can get to the brain first, I might be able to use my symbioid to stop the Rel."

"By the time we get to the brain stem, past all of that," his gaze flickered to the raging battle below, "it may be too late. I will not risk your world or mine to save these people."

"Captain … Mallel, if we survive this coming battle … are we just going to have to kill each other?"

Mallel was silent for a moment. "Tara, it's just you and me against evil. We may not get that far." He smiled sadly. "Let us cross that bridge when we come to it."

She smiled wanly back. "Then what's our plan, Captain?"

Below, a fresh gondola smashed into the breach, breaking the phalanx of Custanguin apart. The masses of Slithmet and war parties teemed in after it.

"I say we follow in Hoztic's footsteps and ride this thing into the breach." Mallel chuckled. "Because time is against us."

Tara nodded, feeling her Luck Symbioid spike. She knew she might survive … but Mallel might not … "Ignite your energy cutlass, Captain. We can use the magnetic pull it creates to steer this thing."

"Help me hold onto it," Mallel said as he drew his cutlass.

Tara gripped the hilt over his hand as he ignited the switch, and brimming energy surged throughout the blade. The two were nearly torn from their little raft, but held firm. They directed the cutlass towards the breach in the skull, and the mad-dash tumble of their little vessel evened out to a wild pirouetting as they struggled to aim.

They weren't going to hit the breach … they were going to smash into the skull itself.

The tingling spiked violently. Would her luck save her and put Mallel in danger?

I want him … she started to think, as she shut her eyes and waited for the impact. She commanded the Luck Symbioid to act on his behalf as well as hers. She *needed* him to survive, even though they may come to blows after the battle was done. She ignored that possibility and grabbed onto Mallel with her free arm while he gripped the raft with his. The stars whirled around them, occasionally obscured by the behemoth body of the Beast as their little transport whirled and whirled faster and faster.

And all Tara could think of while they hurtled to their doom was *I want Mallel!*

There was a titanic boom and the world shuddered. Mallel's arm wrapped around her; it was so large and powerful, keeping her safe.

But also keep HIM safe! Tara pleaded with the Luck Symbioid. "Please!" she screamed as rock crunched under stone and light turned to dark.

The raft shattered through the cracking skull plate and smashed into the honeycombed innards of the interior bone. It ricocheted off a pillar-like structure and buried into a viscous goop with the consistency of a damp, shredded sponge.

The raft slowed to a drift with a *schlurp* and tumbled out the other side of what Tara could only assume was some kind of marrow, and then tumbled—gently—to a stop.

"What in the Three Perversities was that?" Tara spat a fleck of red goop from her lips.

"Hrnnnn?" Mallel groaned. "I think we died?" he finally managed to say. He was still gripping the sword and her.

Tara wrestled out of his vise-like embrace and took his face in her hands, pressing her forehead into his. "Are you all right?"

She blinked away the goop and debris from the crash. Their raft was shattered into pieces around them. She looked into his dark eyes; they took a moment to refocus before they locked with hers.

"Are ..." Her lip quivered. "Are you all right?"

"I'm ... I'm all right." He coughed and spluttered.

"Hoztic survived." Tara narrowed her eyes, releasing Mallel's face and pulling herself onto her feet.

Ahead of them was the gondola that had breached the phalanx of Custanguin. There was a vicious brawl around it between the impossible creatures as more war bands poured in behind them.

Tara tried to get her bearings before she leaped into the fray.

They stood upon a plate of somewhat solid ground, gazing out into the skull cavity, which caused Tara's breath to stifle in her lungs with its gargantuan beauty.

If they were in a building, Tara would have described it like a pavilion. It was a large, round, open space that tapered into a blunt point at the top. The area was lit by bundles of sinew that spread out from a central dome in the ground, most of which were spilling down a ridged fissure that ran through the middle of the cavernous space. Pulses of light shot through these bundles like thunderbolts.

"Nerves?" Mallel thought aloud.

But Tara's eyes were on the squadrons of Custanguin that were thundering into the fray.

They were charging to fill the breach in the defences left by the rampaging gondola. But even as they rushed to the breach and even as they managed to halt the storming war parties, the Slithmet in their metallic siren suits wormed their way into the honeycombed structure inside of the skull plate. They breached out of the viscous goop from the ceiling and massed behind the defenders as they were distracted by the war bands, pirates, marauders, and biological looters from the orbiting worlds.

Cronetta Lesh was among the war band. She weaved and danced her way through the legs and feet of the stomping behemoths to reconnect with the group of Slithmet who now stood off against two inert Custanguin by the central dome. These two were larger than the rest, guarding some kind of door.

Tara's gaze followed Cronetta's path, homing in on the little parcel she had under her arm.

"She made a device from my bombs!" Tara hissed. "We aren't going to be able to stop them."

Mallel took her hand in his. "Hey, we have to try."

Tara set her jaw and nodded, pulling her scarf up over her mouth once more and drawing her knives. "After you."

Mallel smirked and ignited his energy cutlass. Here within these walls, it was not torn from his grip. He leaped over forward and dashed towards the melee with Tara in his wake.

It was relatively easy to get through the warring parties. The war band was getting smashed to bits and was being forced back through the breach. But more Slithmet were slithering out of the bone marrow around the battle that occupied the Custanguin.

The difficulty came after they broke through the melee.

They dashed across the cavernous space towards the Slithmet who were squaring off against the two larger Custanguin. Cronetta—having handed off her explosive device—turned to face them.

She smiled a devilish, fanged greeting from under her large hat. Her rope dart hung limply in one hand. "So you lot keep surviving?" she said as the Slithmet engaged the two Custanguin behind her.

These two Custanguin were stronger, larger, and faster than the Slithmet. It seemed an easy contest, but the attacking forces enwrapped the Custanguin with their tails like ropes while their comrades slithered into their joints. They jabbed and slashed at sinew with claw and fang.

Hoztic stayed on the outskirts with several bodyguards and the parcel under his taloned grip. All he had to do was wait.

Cronetta started whirling her rope dart; it whistled through the air as she snarled, "Shall we dance one last time, little bounty hunter? Let the best woman claim this man as a prize?" She nodded at Mallel.

"I'm not yours for the taking," Mallel growled.

The strobing neurons flashed in the whirling blade of the rope dart, and Cronetta smirked. "Hush, lover, the killers are talking."

With a wide arch she whirled her arm around her head and lashed out with the rope dart, which Mallel barely dodged. The blade cut through his cheek, and blue blood spilled down his face as he gasped.

"You dare!" Tara launched forward and threw one of her knives.

Cronetta drew back her dart and deflected the blade with a flick and then lashed out at Tara's feet.

Tara dived over the tripping blow and rolled over her shoulder as she drew a spare smoke bomb from her pocket. She lobbed it, aiming for Cronetta's face. The bomb flew straight, and acting on reflex Cronetta drew her dart back and bashed it away. As she deflected the smoke bomb, it exploded before her face. Cronetta rocked back, coughing and hacking as Tara slinked in and pounced on her, knife underhanded, intending to stab Cronetta in the ear.

In a flash of dissipating smoke, Tara was on top of the bounty hunter. But Cronetta managed to wrap Tara's attacking arm in loops of her rope dart while rolling to the side. Coughing and heaving, she grappled Tara upon a nerve bundle, rolling closer to the chasm of the spinal cord.

Cronetta got a loop around Tara's neck in the brawl, and in their sprawl they stopped with Tara's head over the edge of the chasm. The nerves pulsated beneath, and the cavernous skull yawned above as Cronetta pinned her in place, snarling in the under-lit strobing light.

"You were good, I'll admit that!" Cronetta pulled the rope tighter around Tara's neck. All Tara could do was reach for another throwing knife, but Cronetta jammed her stiletto into Tara's arm and kept it pinned there. "But you just weren't good enough, offworlder!" She yanked the rope even tighter, and Tara choked, her vision filling with red and black spots as the ringing intensified in her ears and the pressure built in her brain.

But with the rising pressure, her Luck Symbioid flared louder in her mind.

She noticed a shape moving to head them off—was it Mallel? But if he came to save Tara, his back would be turned on the idle Slithmet who were watching their duel with interest.

No! Tara screamed in her dying mind. *Do not save me at the expense of him!*

Mallel seemed to realise the Slithmet were advancing on him, and he was forced to do battle with them rather than save Tara.

Thank you!

She tried to strike at Cronetta, but her opponent just hissed in laughter at the feeble attempt.

The tingling hurt now, like someone was bashing a gong in her head, adding to the pain of being strangled, adding to the horror of Coretta's under-lit sneer. It was as if she could hear the Luck Symbioid screaming at her, *Just use me!*

And so she acquiesced.

As her world went dark, there was a final, bright, blinding light.

CHAPTER 18

Snipes

"What do you mean we're drifting tailwards?" the technician yelled while hunched over his data pad.

"I mean no matter how much thrust we exert, we're gonna keep drifting tailwards after the initial burst cuts out!" the second techie responded.

Snipes was massaging his forehead during the escalating exchange. He had a nasty bump forming above his eye, and he could feel his heart throbbing through it with every beat. "Gentlemen!" he snapped. "Why not just keep thrusting continuously then?"

The two techies looked at him in stunned silence; Snipes wondered why, as he didn't think his idea was particularly revolutionary.

"Did you hit your head or something, Stemcog?"

"Yes," Snipes hissed, removing the cool rag from his throbbing head wound. "The same as everyone else on this ship when we were ... expelled from the anus. So how about we cool our boilers and keep the snarkiness to a minimum? We've all had an extremely rough few days."

"Our thrust won't burn long enough; the solar sail is a mess," the first techie responded. "And we can't seem to get caught in the Beast's gravitational pull for some reason; our magnetic resonance is counter to the Beast's, which pushes us back. Which basically means we can only get so far before we run out of power, and if we wait long enough for a decent charge, we'll drift too far away. We'll slip out of the influence of the Beast's propulsion, and by the time we can blink, we'll see it speed forward and devour our worlds."

Snipes regarded the blinking lights on one of the few un-shattered screens on the ruined bridge. It showed what was explained to him as a readout of all of the different crew members who were spread out in and around the Beast's superstructure and orbiting worlds. They would go and round them up eventually, but now that they had jettisoned from inside the Beast, they were able to intercept a repeating message. It was the conversation between Votly and Mallel. They didn't have time to round up the stragglers; they needed to get to the skull, and fast.

One of the red dots represented Tara, he was sure. The one representing Flayr was weak within the bowels of the Beast, and a large cluster of signals was located by the Beast's fin.

"Can we get to the majority of points at least?" Snipes asked, gesturing to the signal cluster.

"We can, but a good number of them are riflemen." The techie eyed the only remaining rifleman on the bridge, who was flanked by several marines. The rifleman eyed the techie back sheepishly.

"We didn't know the Slithmet were in league with the Rel," the rifleman pleaded. "If we did we never would have ..."

"Betrayed your own kind?" One of the marines stepped in to smash him with the butt of his prism rifle.

"Oi!" Snipes roared, and regretted it immediately as his head throbbed. He gasped and struggled to catch his footing.

"You really should see the medic," the techie said.

"I would but she's busy with all of the other injured people. Some who were injured when you lot were fighting the Custanguin, some from when you were fighting each other, and do you want to know what I noticed about that? I noticed there were far fewer casualties when you lot were working together."

"How can we trust the riflemen though, Stemcog?" a marine asked.

"Because that conversation between Votly and Mallel made it clear that the riflemen were right stupid bastards, and I'm sure they feel very foolish about leading a coup with the help of the Rel, which they were sworn to defeat." Snipes cocked his head at the rifleman, who nodded guiltily and looked down at his feet. "Now we need to get to the skull to back up the captain and Tara. But there are only five battle-ready people on this boat, and if we go in like we are now, we're going to get diced up pretty quick. We need those fighters, and maybe there are techies there to help us get the *Motebeam* worthy enough that we can make it there in one piece. You lot can sort out your differences *after* we save both of our worlds from certain destruction. We all saw what that Beast did to that planet on the edge of our sun well; our people need us to cool our boilers. So let's cool them and get to work!"

Snipes gasped again as the world spun beneath his feet, and he almost fainted. An arm grabbed him by the shoulder and hauled him up; once Snipes blinked through his confusion, he realised it was the rifleman who had caught him.

"I acted in defiance of my captain with full knowledge of what I was doing, and will accept the consequences of my actions. Many from my ranks will agree with me ... We were angry, that's all. We thought the captain only brought the woven assassin on board because he liked her ... She killed our friends, and yes, I understand we struck first. It's just, a lot ..."

"I know." Snipes grabbed his arms. "And you will face consequences for your actions, I'm sure, but at least you can swallow your pride to save our worlds. Now, let's go. Can we get enough juice in the engine to get us to that cluster?" he asked the techie.

The tech furrowed his brow, and then he nodded tensely. "Here goes nothing."

* * *

Votly

Votly trudged out of the armpit of the Beast, leading an assortment of beleaguered marines who were flanking riflemen whose wrists were still bound. The marines themselves were flanked again by Culs and Ekelts on either side of their column.

"Which way to the skull?" Votly fretted, trying desperately to repair her burned-out Light Gauntlet with a bent screwdriver and a cracked replacement lens. She had taken the pistol from Keihn and inserted its prism into the upper part of her gauntlet. She had an idea ... but she wasn't sure if it would work.

"That way, my king." A Cul pointed upwards. "It will take us several days to get there." The Beast's great mass ebbed up and down on the horizon, and two little dots twinkled in the distance, growing larger.

"We don't have days. We probably don't even have hours," Votly lamented.

"Look!" Curla pointed with an energy cutlass she took from a rifleman. "It's the *Motebeam*!"

Votly spun tailwards so fast that she slipped and fell, only to bounce into the pudgy, calloused belly of the Cul and land back on her feet. The sad silhouette of the marred and punctured *Motebeam* drifted into view, listing on one side. The chrome hull was dented and torn almost to shreds, and the solar sails were crumpled as if they had been chewed on. But they still pulsed weakly, and it still drifted closer.

"Thank the Prismatists for that!" Votly whimpered as the marines and even some riflemen cheered alongside each other.

* * *

It was an awkward affair to board the *Motebeam*.

There was sporadic radio communication that came through from it in clipped bursts. Whenever the *Motebeam* propelled itself over the mismatched party, it would start drifting tailwards immediately. It wouldn't dare land in case it couldn't summon the power to propel itself upwards again. Instead it would just drag back along the jagged peaks of the spine, chipping away chunks that scattered into the void.

Votly realised that this was due to the fact the ship's magnetic resonance was in constant antagonistic relationship with the Beast, something that must have happened when it smashed into the skull in half Wave-Form ...

Curla had the idea to get the crew to open the loading bay rampart at the back and drop off a *raft* of sorts that was tethered by chains.

"Okay," the techie onboard the *Motebeam* rasped into the receiver on the bridge. There was a keen ringing feedback which made the Prismath on the Beast's surface wince. "We've only got enough juice for one more thrust; you're going to have to make this count!"

Votly turned to her marines and gestured to the riflemen. "Untie them."

There was an uneasy muttering.

"Hey," she turned and snapped, "if we don't get as many fighting people onto the *Motebeam* as possible and figure out how to repair it in time to get to the skull, then our world will be munched on by this titanic creature! So snap out of it; we have a common enemy now."

The marines grumblingly obeyed, and Votly explained what was about to happen to the bulk of the Culs and Ekelts, who listened silently in wonder.

"Okay," Curla said, "it's coming in to make the drop-off. Stand back!"

The mishmash group parted as the *Motebeam* swung in overhead. Its back rampart opened. With a scathing slide of chrome upon chrome, a haphazardly assembled raft of panelling, crates, and whatever else was in the cargo bay of the *Motebeam* dropped loose.

It smashed into the surface with a screech, and most of the raft crumbled into dozens of large chunks. Luckily each chunk was secured by its own tether as the *Motebeam* swooped past, dragging the panels across the rocky, skeletal landscape and kicking up bright sparks that fractured in the magnetosphere in a myriad of hypnotising colours.

"Now!" Votly ordered.

The groups on either side of the mad stampede of sparking metal swarmed to grab onto whatever they could. It turned into a mad-dash brawl as Prismath, Ekelt, and Cul all clambered onto each section, hauling each other onto the platforms as they shook uncontrollably.

Votly dived for the platform before her … and missed. She hit the coarse dust that passed for soil in this landscape. She rose up in time to see and duck beneath the next haphazard piece of panelling, and then watched in horror as she realised she couldn't dodge the next one.

One passed by her side, and a hand shot out; it was Curla's. She grabbed Votly bodily by the scruff of her neck and yanked her onto her tiny little panel. Curla got Votly just in time to be carried away as the *Motebeam* gained elevation and started drifting back tailwards.

"Reel us in now!" Votly barked up the chains and tethers. "We don't have much time!"

* * *

It was a relatively successful if somewhat chaotic operation. Votly estimated about 90 percent of their people—including the two native tribes—managed to get reeled up into the cargo hold of the *Motebeam* as it lost propulsion and started drifting back down the spine of the Beast towards the whipping tail.

"What turned my *Dustmote* into shards?" Votly panted as one of the crewmen pulled her onto her feet and she gazed around the marred chrome interior.

"Ah, Votly, we've been through *a lot*, even before the *Motebeam* was Wave-Form rammed into this living celestial object!" the crewman said. "Now the techies need you on the bridge."

"Right." Votly turned to Curla, who was corralling the riflemen back into a line against the far wall of the hold. "Curla, I want you to organise our forces. Ready landing parties and get our cannons manned."

"I don't have enough people to man the cannons *and* form boarding parties, even with the creatures you bought on board with us," Curla said.

"Arm the riflemen." The cargo hold went still as the loading ramp groaned into place. "Are your lenses smudged?" Votly shrieked. "If we don't stop the Rel *now*, then all is lost. And I swear to the High Prismatists of old, if any of you mutineers do a mutiny in the next half an hour, I am going to jettison you out of the hold into the maws of this giant Beast. Am I understood?"

There was a muted shuffling.

Votly's temper spiked. "That was not a rhetorical question!"

"You're understood," one of the riflemen said.

"We understand," Curla answered almost at the same time.

"Good." Votly turned to the Ekelts and Culs. "Curla," she pointed, "is my second in command; any order from her is as good as an order from me."

The Ekelts and Culs nodded and bowed. "Yes, King," one said.

Votly grabbed one of the techies and bolted from the cargo hold, beckoning him to give a panting damage report as they tore down the chrome corridors.

As she left the hold, she overheard whispered conversation from some of the crew members who were already on the *Motebeam.* "When did she find that backbone?"

"She killed Keihn in single combat ..." someone else replied, before they were too far out of earshot.

* * *

Snipes

Votly burst into the battle-scarred bridge. Two techies, a few marines, and rifleman turned in a start to watch her.

"Votly." Snipes looked up from a readout on one of the few undamaged consoles. "Do you know how to get this ship to the skull?"

Votly stalked in, scanning the bridge for her console. She went to it and gathered equipment from her drawer to insert into her Light Gauntlet. Then she tapped away at her device as fresh holographic readouts of the ship flitted through her vision.

"Yes," she answered Snipes, "but not for a few days. We've already drifted so far back that the Beast will swim us by, and we'll be stranded while Mallel and Tara fight the Rel and the Slithmet alone."

216

"Then what do we do?" Snipes asked.

"There is the Wave-Form engine ... it seems to still be working. But it would be like bringing a boat into dock while riding a tidal wave. And there's too much magnetic interference; there's too many orbiting bodies and gravitational pulls. We couldn't get a straight shot."

Snipes perked up. "Is magnetic interference something that would pull us off course? Like gravity pulling a bullet towards the ground?"

"Yes?"

"I can aim us," Snipes said. "I can aim us like I would line up a shot, and you can pull the trigger, getting us to the base of the skull in an instant." Snipes licked his lips, his brow furrowing as he tried to visualise the feat.

"But, but, Snipes!" Votly cried. "There are too many variables, too many orbiting worlds, too many shifts in the magnetic field as the Beast swims."

"Get me a readout ..." Snipes gestured Votly to the console "... that shows me all of the gravitational pulls as the worlds orbit the Beast, that shows me the undulation in the magnetic currents as it swims, and readouts that show how these things will affect our path as we fly through in Wave-Form. I will line up the ship and steer it as we launch."

"But we'll be in Wave-Form!" Votly said. "You couldn't even stand on your own two feet because the floor was pulsating too much. How can you do it?"

"Because I was inside that creature after the *Motebeam* stranded me there. I fought in the unstable grounds of its stomach against a cancer ... I can do this, Votly."

"Okay, you line up the shot, then strap yourself in. When we hit the base of the skull ... well, we're going to be ramming it ... again."

"No," Snipes said, "I have to stay here, steering the ship, in case there are surprise changes in our trajectory I'll have to correct mid-flight."

"But, Snipes, you'll have less than split seconds to react, and when we stop ..."

"I'll be fine, Votly. We have to get there, no matter the risk." Snipes breathed hard. "This is how I atone for my sins. I'm ready."

"Okay," Votly nodded, "but when we impact, you hold on for dear life!"

"I will, I promise."

Votly issued orders to the others on the bridge and then made a ship-wide announcement. "All crew members and warriors, prepare for Wave-Form jump. We're going to be coming into a live battlefield, so prepare for anything."

"Is she crazy?" one of the techies whispered.

"No." Snipes stepped up to the helm as Votly set up the readouts and displays that he needed. "I am."

The Wave-Form engine started to thrum. Snipes's heart rate spiked, and his breaths became shallow. He grounded his feet and forced himself to take a deep breath as he gazed out the bridge view screen.

The entire length of the Beast was now almost spread out before them, rising and falling in a rhythmic motion. The overlay of all the different magnetic forces was layered on top of it so that Snipes could trace a path as the *Motebeam* tore over it within fractions of a section. Then the readout showed the pull of different gravitational fields from the different orbiting worlds that revolved around the Beast in a spiralling fashion.

There were hundreds of red and blue lines and arrows. A torrent of information that looked like coloured flakes of snow in a blizzard. They all overlayed the impossible form of the titanic Beast as it made its way between the stars.

"Okay," Snipes directed the ship by the helm.

A green line traced their predicted path through the maelstrom, arching over undulating peaks, troughs, and through the orbiting worlds that crested or fell below the horizons.

The green line constantly shifted and scattered, and Snipes kept adjusting the pitch of the *Motebeam*, never able to find a clear path for more than a second.

"I'm going to call out as soon as the shot is lined up," Snipes said. "As soon as the engine fires, we'll be off course again ... I'll definitely have to adjust mid-flight." Sweat was pouring down his brow, his teeth were clenched, and his heart was hammering harder in his chest.

I can do this, he thought. *This is why I came out here, to atone ... Even if the world crumbles around me, I am unshakable.*

"What if you miss?" Votly strapped herself in with her hand on the Wave-Form ignition, ready to push it the instant Snipes said.

"I won't."

Snipes took one last breath as the green line—ebbing and flowing through the magnetic, gravitational, and physical chaos—ended at the base of the skull in an unbroken path.

"Fire!"

Votly hit the button, the Wave-Form engine thrummed as it revved, and the ground pulsed and fluctuated beneath Snipe's feet.

He ignored it, focusing only on his goal.

The thrumming engine reached a crescendo, and the *Motebeam* launched in a flaring blaze of colour. The green line in Snipe's vision shifted through the eddying chaos so wildly that they would shoot past the Beast and into the sun. In the split second he had to react, he shifted the helm, and as he realised what was about to happen, he clenched his eyes shut.

CHAPTER 19

Tara Star

Tara thought the bright light was her oncoming death; she didn't expect it to be accompanied by an explosion of sound and a showering of bony marrow-flecked debris. She always expected death to slide over you like a clinging film—if she were so lucky to die peacefully, that was—but this ... this was too much.

It was as if a surge of sensations were shooting through her, light, pain, sound ... until she realised it was because the noose had loosened around her neck, that she had taken a desperate breath of air, and that Cronetta had been partially dislodged from her dominant position. Her enemy was distracted, so Tara took advantage of that despite her pain and despite her curiosity at what cataclysm had saved her.

She jabbed out, hard, and Cronetta's nose crunched from the force of her bare knuckles.

Taking further advantage of her disorientation, Tara shot her hips up and toppled Cronetta from her perch. Tara rolled while pulling the rope dart from her neck. She gained a position on top of Cronetta and now wrapped the rope dart around her neck instead.

Tara yanked the cord tight, standing and hauling Cronetta to her feet. "You should have killed me when you had the chance!" Tara kicked Cronetta into the chasm of the spinal cord.

Cronetta grunted and tumbled, bashing into the first plate of the vertebrae as she fell into the strobe-lit abyss. Tara grabbed hold of the rope dart with all her might. The rope went taut with a sickening snap and yank that nearly tore out her arm sockets.

Tara spat blood from her teeth and yanked on the rope again. Her Luck Symbioid tingled, and the rope came loose from Cronetta's broken neck.

The once fearsome bounty hunter tumbled lifelessly into a pool of spinal fluid and was carried away in the shooting nerves. Tara allowed herself to take in the surrounding scene as she pulled the rope dart up and wrapped it around her torso, ready to use in the coming fight.

She wasn't sure if she was hallucinating or not: the thing that had saved her was the *Motebeam*.

It had burst through the break in the Beast's skull like a blazing comet and was unloading the full might of its cannons upon the Slithmet and the rival war parties in a brilliant display of light and power.

For an instant, Tara was taken back to when she was in Crankod, to when she first saw the sheer terrifying might of the Light Wizards as they destroyed that poor city. Now the ship was crumpled, ruined, and firing a broadside as it listed to one side … but it *was* on her side.

The loading rampart opened at the back, and a combined force of marines, riflemen, and strange creatures poured out to fight off the enemy who were seeking shelter beneath the field of fire of the cannons.

The force was led by "… Votly?" Tara cocked her head.

"Drive off the shards!" Votly shrieked. She raised her Light Gauntlet and pulled a trigger on the mechanism. A powerful beam of light sheared a Slithmet in half, and the exoskeleton was mobbed by half a dozen pudgy aliens before the gangly creature that piloted it could escape. "Rally to Tara and the captain!"

"The captain … Mallel!" Tara turned to find the Slithmet had formed a defensive circle around the central node in the skull cavity.

Mallel had his blade drawn and powered on, trading swipes and dodges with the two Slithmet who had stopped him from saving her.

Without a moment's hesitation Tara leaped forward with a scream of fury. She unfurled the rope dart from around her torso in a swinging motion and whipped it out, aiming for the closest Slithmet's eye. She had trained with a rope dart during her assassin years and had done quite well with it, only it lacked the practicality of a concealed throwing knife in stealthy situations.

In the years since then, her skill had withered somewhat, but the blade pinged off the Slithmet's skull and distracted it enough for her to close the distance and roll around the base of its slithering tail.

She looped the rope dart around its neck and pulled down, kicking up to plant her boot into its jaw as she yanked the Slithmet down with all her might. Under the force of her blow, the fangs within the jaw cracked and the Slithmet grunted.

Tara darted back, whipped the rope dart free, and swung it underhand to whip up and crack the creature in the jaw again. The faceplate split open and hung limply as the Slithmet roared in anguish. Tara leaped up its torso, snapping the rope dart back to grip the blade like a dagger, and reached into the limply hanging jaw. The Slithmet screamed. She drove her knife deep into the innards until it struck something soft—the fleshy part of the creature that piloted the exoskeleton.

The Slithmet gasped and collapsed dead. Tara wrenched the rope dart out, turning to help Mallel. He was drawing his energy blade from a gap he had ripped open in his foe's chest plating.

"You're alive!" He rushed forward and took her in his arms.

"So are you." She reached up to take his cheek, but her tingling spiked.

Not yet, the tingling was telling her.

She pulled back and turned to the Slithmet who were guarding the central node; the two larger Custanguin lay in broken ruins. There were a dozen remaining Slithmet, and they were clustering together, slithering and sliding over one another in a shower of sparks and light. Plate fused to plate and heads joined together as the many formed into one.

"Are they combining?" Mallel asked.

"Yep," Tara spun her new rope dart in anticipation, "but so are we."

Votly and her mismatched band of warriors charged around the spinal chasm en masse.

"Captain!" she cried, rushing forward. "I have assembled what fighters we have available, sir." She saluted; her nose was broken, and her peach skin face was marred by grime, filth, and a myriad of different-coloured blood.

"Votly," Mallel said quietly, "what happened to you?"

Votly's eyes flickered for a moment, welling with moisture that threatened to spill out over her cheeks. "With respect, Captain, that can wait. We have monsters to fight."

"Oh?" Mallel broke his authoritative air for a split second before righting himself. "Correct, Miss Votly." He turned back to the Slithmet.

Twelve separate exoskeletons were now joined to form a horrid-looking creature. An enormous being with two legs formed from several wound Slithmet tails. It was spined with sharp spokes and had an assortment of different limbs armed with claws and scythes. Red eyes littered the body in connective places, but the head was a nightmarish visage of three different heads forming an enormous, disjointed maw with rows upon rows of teeth. The joints where each different exoskeleton connected writhed with black sinew, and when Tara noticed them, her Luck and Master Symbioids tingled.

At the central skull dome behind the combined monster, Hoztic set the bomb that Cronetta had provided and scurried away.

The Slithmet monstrosity spoke, twelve voices overlaying to create an unsettling, distorted effect. "We are the Slithmet," it said, "and scions of The Rel. This creature will be ours, and your worlds will suffer for it."

One of the pudgy, calloused aliens that arrived with Votly roared, "Your kind has made ours suffer enough. Our king will make you pay!" It charged forward with a brutal war cry—a large iron club in one hand—and the Slithmet beast slashed down at it with an assortment of sharp limbs that formed a spiked whip.

The Cul was cut to shreds.

"Prism rifles!" Mallel ordered.

Two scores of Prism rifles opened fire on the Slithmet monster, each beam pinging uselessly off its carapace.

"Can we use the *Motebeam*?" Tara flinched as the Slithmet laughed and stepped forward. Behind it, the bomb went off, leaving a smouldering, cracked opening after a bright flash. Hoztic's exoskeleton opened at the chest, and his frail form scuttled out of it, slipping inside. "We need to stop Hoztic, now!"

"We can't use the cannons!" Votly shouted, flicking through readouts on her Light Gauntlet. "We could cause irreparable damage to the brain stem. We only used the cannons to fire on the clumps of enemies we knew we could hit without issue. But I've overcharged my Light Gauntlet. If I can get a direct hit on its head, I can disorient it, but I don't know what that will do!"

"Use the cannons," Mallel ordered.

"No!" Tara cried. "We cannot kill the Beast!" She shot Mallel a pointed look. "Distract it; get Votly to use her gauntlet."

The Slithmet monster charged forward and slashed at a swathe of its attackers, who scattered and ran. The riflemen scattered and fired haphazardly as the marines split into small squadrons, opening fire at the joints and eyes wherever they could find them. It did nothing. The Ekelts and Culs threw themselves at the monster, clambering over it to do individual battle with each limb and spike that reacted to their presence as if they were their own entity.

"Tara, we don't have time," Mallel hissed.

"Then make time!" Tara pleaded. "Let me get in close and use the Master Symbioid to disrupt their bond. The Slithmet will crumble into individual pieces, and you can mop up what is left. While that's going on, I can stop Hoztic."

"Tara!" Mallel clenched his jaw, and his grip tightened around his blade. "Fine, I will distract it. Votly, when it is looking at me with its maw, let it have it from your weapon. Then, Tara, you do your thing."

"Roger that, Captain." Votly pulled a mechanism back on her Light Gauntlet, and three lenses slid into place along a track before a prism. "Let's slaughter this thing!"

Mallel exchanged a fleeting, surprised glance with Tara—who widened her eyes in surprise—and then he dashed forward.

The Prismath fighters parted ways for him as he roared, energy cutlass flaring in one hand as he struck at the leg of the Slithmet construct. The power of the blow sent a clang through the creature, and it turned to regard him with its many sinister eyes.

"Captain Mallel!" it roared. "You will be the downfall of your race!"

It surged after him and Mallel stood his ground. He ducked under its tail swipe, dodging to one side as a huge spike from an overarching shoulder limb embedded into the ground. Mallel was finally knocked back by a kicking blow from the enormous, studded legs.

Mallel was floored, his sword skittering away from his grasp, but the marines rallied around him. They fired up at the construct's head with a sustained volley. It weathered the fire and deftly swiped at the barrels of their weapons, crushing, snapping, or ripping them from the marines' hands as they were knocked back by the force.

"Puny things," the Slithmet said as it plucked a Cul from its face and used it to bat away an Ekelt. "You will all be consumed; you will all be destroyed!"

Its maw opened wide—impossibly wide—and it leaned down to clamp its jaws around Mallel's winded form.

That's when Votly charged in with a high-pitched cry and stuck her whole arm up into the surprised beast's maw. "Not if you're destroyed first!" she spat, and ignited her weapon.

The prism whined and fired through her first focusing lens. The lens heated white hot, and the power shot out into the second lens, which heated until it was orange hot. The power then shot into the third lens, which burned so brightly that a myriad of colours cascaded over the lens's surface before it exploded in a directed blast of light and power.

The Slithmet's skull exploded outwards. The construct stumbled back with a choir's cry of pain that made all but the most staunch of warriors cower and cover their ears. Votly fell on top of Mallel—her arm a burned crisp. Mallel grabbed her in his arms and turned to shield her from the molten flecks that were falling from the Slithmet's skull.

But even as it screamed and stumbled, black sinews of the Rel were working to weave the exploded mess back together.

Tara took her opportunity and charged forward. Sensing her presence, the Slithmet stumbled further away in uncertainty. But Tara lashed out with her new rope dart, and it embedded in the closing wound of the face plates. She yanked—not strong enough to pull the monster towards her, but hard enough to help her leap up its body and shove her free hand into the connected pieces.

Her symbioid—the Master Symbioid, the one she had unknowingly joined with that fateful day back in Masonville, the one that let her repel Rella's influence in Copper Cobble—did her bidding. The pale sinews shot from her skin and entwined with the Rel's dark barbs. They recoiled at its presence, the Master Symbioid overpowering them and forcing them to retreat from the conjoining parts of the Slithmet, forcing them to crumble apart.

Tara blinked as her mind was partially drawn into the sinewy battle, but she kept a hold on where she was.

The conglomerate monster crumbled into component parts, and Tara leaped back, flipping over to land on her feet as twelve Slithmet landed in a pile. Some were dead from Votly's attack, but the survivors were now exposed as individuals.

"Don't give them time to rejoin!" Tara cried to the marines and riflemen, who rushed in to stab and club and shoot at point-blank range.

They were joined by the Culs and Ekelts in a brutal melee.

The Slithmet resisted in their dazed state, but they would soon be overwhelmed, just not soon enough for Tara to wait and make sure.

She still had one more foe to defeat.

She took one look at Mallel, who was tending to Votly—who was barely conscious and babbled incoherently—and then bolted towards the central skull dome. She scurried around Hoztic's inert exoskeleton and went to the smouldering crack that had been made by her own bombs.

"Tara!" Mallel had left Votly and caught up to her. He had taken up his sword.

"Mallel," she turned, "I can save this creature and everyone who lives on it."

"How? Just tell me how and I'll believe you."

"With the Master Symbioid. If it can repel the Rel, maybe it can influence this creature."

"But you don't know how to use it; you've resisted using your symbioids this whole time. What's changed now?"

"Now I have no choice," she said quietly.

Her eyes drifted to his sword, and despite her feelings for him, she knew he would fight her if he deemed it necessary to save his people. At the thought her Luck Symbioid flared, begging her to trust it, to trust Mallel ...

She sighed. "Will you trust me to save your people?" she asked, her hands by her side.

He looked at her a moment, the fighting still raging behind him, and then he raised his sword. Tara made no move to stop him.

He struck a half-dead Slithmet that was crawling up to her feet.

It died with a rattling hiss.

"Go," he said. "Be the hero I could not. I will guard the entrance and follow when I can."

Tara took a deep, shaky breath, "Thank you," and turned from him, scurrying into the crack in the central dome.

CHAPTER 20

Tara Star

The breach in the central skull node was minor, a smoking crack at the base of the dome, which was marred by scorch marks and littered with chunks of broken metallic matter. Without hesitation Tara dashed into the tiny crawlspace, her scarf keeping the worst of the smoke from stifling her, and shimmied and twisted through the jagged gap that the Slithmet had made, ignoring the sounds of the dying conflict behind her.

Hoztic was slighter than she was, smaller, more wiry, and better suited to crawl into small spaces. That's what his people did to pilot those Slithmet suits after all. But Tara had squeezed through her share of crawlspaces; she wouldn't dare consider what would happen if she could not make it through this one in time.

Ahead of her there was a cry like a guttural grunt, then the sound of something plunging into viscous gloop.

Gritting her teeth, Tara writhed and yanked and pushed through the crawlspace until she emerged into a darkened little dome. It was no bigger than the bridge of the *Motebeam*. The ceiling was smooth and curved down to meet the floor by the little crawlspace Tara emerged from. In the middle of the dome was a well-like depression that took up half of the centre, and within it was what looked like a super cluster of little pink vines. They wrapped and tangled and constricted upon one another in tight bundles. There must have been thousands of strands, and millions—or perhaps infinite—little crevices and folds. The pink matter pulsed blue in erratic patterns as the bundles and clumps filtered into little conduits that spilled out of the well and burrowed into the outer bone wall. The pulses shot along the conduits like energy through power lines.

Some pulses even travelled back into the well as well.

This was the brain.

A decrepit figure was hunched over the brain well, silhouetted by the pulses of light. It was Hoztic.

"Get back!" Tara stepped forward, holding the rope dart blade underhanded. "Your mission has failed, Hoztic. I won't let the Rel take over this creature."

Hoztic sheepishly looked up at her, crystalline grey eyes full of sorrow. He straightened with a grunt, revealing his own claw embedded in his gut.

"What?" Tara hesitated.

"The Rel Scion ..." Hoztic groaned and collapsed forward. "It was screaming in my mind. Get to the brain, let it destroy all living things … foolish, really, in a moment of doubt, asked if it meant the Slithmet too."

Tara rolled her eyes. "Of course it did, you sadistic idiot!" She stepped around Hoztic's prone form carefully. "But at least you stopped yourself before it took hold of you and entered the brain."

Hoztic stifled a pained laugh. "I would not take my own life so readily … I tried to pull back from the brain … The Rel didn't like that …" His voice was fading, and dirty green goo oozed from his stomach.

"What did you do?" Tara was scanning the dome desperately, looking for the slither of the Rel Scion. "Where is the Rel?"

Hoztic pointed a claw towards the brain well. "It made me stab myself, and now it's worming its way into the brain stem … You're too late, Tara … For what it's worth, I'm sorry, for being such a damned fool. As it left me, it told me everything in its malice … It promised us that we could rule over the Great One once it had its revenge. Instead it was going to leave it to die out here in the abyss, far away from sustaining nebula to feed upon.

"It was the Rel's initial invasion that directed the Great One in the first place. The Rel targeted its glands to coerce it to places it wouldn't ordinarily go. But the Custanguin were able to suppress the Rel before it wormed too deeply into its system … and you've seen the rest, scarcity, war, sickness. All of that, all of this, just to bring this Beast to your world … Why are you so special, Tara? What makes your people's death worth the suffering of untold millions?"

Tara was only half focusing on him, her eyes desperately scanning the brain bundles for signs of the sickly little parasite worming its way inside, but that last question caught her off guard. She had killed Rella ... twice ... kind of. But he was just a Scion. Why would the Rel react so vengefully to that? What did make her so special? Then she thought of the Symbioids, and how they inhabited the moons guarding their worlds ... There must have been something in that, surely ...

"I don't know," Tara finally said. She looked at Hoztic, who had passed away while she fretted and pondered, "but I will make the Rel pay for what it's done, Hoztic, I promise."

Tara turned from Hoztic's wretched corpse and knelt down by the brain well, placing her hands gently on the bundles. The brain trembled beneath her touch.

"How?" she asked. "How can I save you?"

She knew the answer; she just wasn't sure she wanted to do it. Within her she had two symbioids. One was the Luck Symbioid, which she still did not entirely trust to use. Every time it saved her in the past, it was at the detriment of those around her—she harkened back to how she defeated its previous weaver, a deadly bounty hunter who abused his power. She decided that she *didn't* want to kill him; she decided that his good luck was her bad luck, and killing him was bad luck for her. Then, the Luck Symbioid wove with her without her realising, and it saved her again and again, always moving people or things in the way of danger. Poor Regen, atomised to a crisp when he pushed her out of the way of the *Motebeam's* cannons in Crankod ...

But now that she needed it, the tingling was not flaring.

This Beast, this battle, was far too big for even its manipulation of luck.

But she also had the other symbioid, one she wove with by accident—on account of the Luck Symbioid no doubt. The Master Symbioid, used by the Symbicate to rip symbioids from their weavers for decades. It was the one that was able to repel the influence of Rella. She could use it now to weave into the brain of the Beast, to find the Rel and smite it sinew to sinew. But then why wasn't the Luck Symbioid tingling when she had that idea? What was the danger?

Because my mind would have to follow the symbioid down in order to maintain my will over it, she realised, remembering how her mind almost followed the Master Symbioid as it dismantled the Slithmet Construct moments ago. *It won't work on my behalf unless I go in with it. And without me to guide its wrath, who knows what it will do to the Beast in order to defend my home world?*

Her mind quailed, imagining sinking down into the thoughts of this unfathomable titan that had lived for millennia. It could drive her insane ... it could kill her ... and on top of that, she would need to overpower the Rel as well. As small as this Rel Scion was, it was also long-lived, and vicious, and would not go down without a fight.

Then there was the flip side. What if she won, but lost herself in the Beast? What if she lost all semblance of herself except for the Beast's need to feed? And the closest places for it to feed right now were the two worlds that she was trying to save ... Was that why the Luck Symbioid wasn't tingling? Was the danger too great?

"You can do it." It was Mallel.

Tara turned.

Mallel was a mess; he had thrown off his captain's cloak to squeeze through the crawlspace. His shirt was torn and shredded, exposing broad, muscled shoulders that were gashed with the ink-blue blood of his people.

"How do you know? How do you even know the danger?" Tara asked.

"Because I can see why you're hesitating; you're afraid of what you might become. You've always feared your potential for the damage it can inflict ... like me. When I had the power to make a difference, I failed. But you never once consider that the power you wield is wielded by ... well ... you. I believe you will make the right choices, the hard decisions ... You can do it. You have never wavered in your conviction since I have known you, no matter what internal battles you fought. You have always found a way to prevail. You make me want to be a better fighter, a better leader, a better man. If anyone can wield this power, it's you. Direct the Beast away from our worlds, Tara. I will stand watch over you while you do battle."

"You promise?" Tara asked meekly.

"Yes." He stepped forward and placed his hand on her shoulder.

"Do you promise to kill me if I lose control? If I lose myself to the Beast?"

Mallel hesitated. "You know I will do what I must ..."

"But?"

"But I don't want to lose you, Tara," he said, and looked away. "It's selfish of me."

She reached up to his cheek, directing his gaze back to her; she leaned in—hastily pulled down her scarf—and kissed him. "You won't lose me," she whispered. "But be ready …" she stepped back and smiled as a tear rolled down her cheek, "… just in case."

She turned from him—stunned and speechless—and crouched, placing both of her hands on the brain bundles. Her tingling flared, it was unsure, but something else shifted—a symbioid woven deeper into her body—and the tingling shifted too, bowing to the greater power. A warm tendril feeling moved through her arms, and Tara felt as if she was being pulled down through her own limbs as the sinews erupted from her and intertwined with the bundles.

All of a sudden it was like Tara was in free fall, falling past the stars and the universe and all of the planets and people and sights and wonders it contained. She was a giant, a titan of the cosmos, drifting through it with ease and feeding on the rich gasses and liquids of the nebula in the centre of the galaxy. Millennia passed before her like an onrushing river … and then … darkness.

Something slithered through eternity, something wicked. It lashed out of the abyss with a stinging blow and wrapped around Tara … around … someone … and the forces of matter wrestled. Shadow and darkness were resisted with … not lightness.

Sensations flitted in and out of comprehension as the universe unfolded across the ages. The only constant, the only real thing that Tara … no, that … *Who was I?* The thought was like a lance of lightning—fleeting and blinding—but after it faded only one constant remained: it was conflict, it was battle.

The Rel was what slithered from the abyss; it wormed its way into the Beast's mind … into Tara's mind. But something resisted, something made of light and sinew ... the Master Symbioid. The two forces raged against one another while eternity quaked in the Beast-Tara mind, their struggle threatening to destroy nerve and brain and thought.

Tara forced herself into the fray, urging the symbioid not to fight so wantonly. With her to focus its resolve, it ensnared the dark sinew in folds of light, burning it from the abyss.

And then the battle was done. The darkness was ensnared, bound, squeezed, pulped, and strangled into oblivion. The Master Symbioid receded into Tara's mind, but she had not receded from the Beast's. The sinews of Luck beckoned her to leave, but suddenly there was only the universe, the drift through the hazy nebulas ... and hunger, a great hunger as they drifted through the abyss on magnetic eddies.

She was no longer one mind, but four, and one imposed on the rest.

Was that food over there? Two little polyps of rock, liquid, and air blazed in their visions. They would not satiate their hunger, but they would suffice. They swam towards the little morsels of life ...

Life?

Tara felt something squeeze her hand. Instead of floating through the abyss, she was in free fall again. She fell across the insurmountable gulfs of the cosmos, across the awareness of this great, infallible creature. In fear she remembered she was just a woman swimming in the churning waters of a titanic Beast's mind, of the Great One. She could not confound it, could not barter with it or convince it to move away to feed on uninhabited nebula once more. She was just a ...

Her hand, someone was squeezing her hand.

This was not a matter of whether she could, she realised. Her limitations were irrelevant. All that mattered was that the Rel was defeated, and that she was going to save her people ... save Mallel's people too ... save Mallel.

The kiss danced across her mind, and the vast gulf of impossibility shrank. One word came to mind, one command to force the Beast to keel.

TURN!

To say she screamed would not have made sense, but she knew if she could have heard the determined desperation in her voice, it would have made armies quail. It would have made the surging tide recede and the very light of the sun wink and wane. It was not so much a plea or order, but a demand of cosmological force itself. She was no mere street urchin, caught and trained in the arts of death and fumbling through life. She was Tara Star, wielder of the Symdian's last gifts ... and one day, she might actually understand what that meant.

But for now, her defiance against her own destructive fate was enough.

The Beast, pained by hunger, head aching from repeated fevers and blows, groaned silently in the abyss, and it bowed to this new command.

Silently, almost without effort, the two little morsels drifted out of its view, and it focused on a cluster of lights in the distance. These were a real bounty to feast on, only if it waited a little longer.

Tara fell again, fell upwards, backwards, away. She was this infinitesimal speck, a leaf upon the ocean in a hurricane. She, she ...

She fell back onto her arse.

The room spun like a whirlwind; her guts were about to launch up through her head. But among the churning and chaos, a hand held onto hers. It was gentle but firm, calloused yet soft. It could hold her close and caress her fears in the darkest pit of the night, or it could pull her from the sheer snare of gravity itself.

She blinked—eyes red and tear stained—and looked up at her anchor, at Mallel.

He was crouched before her, the pulsating brain well illuminating his face with a soft blue glow; such a concerned face. In his other hand he held his prism pistol low, his finger off the trigger.

"Tara?" he said. "You're here, you're here," he cooed. "Did you do it?"

"Unng," Tara said. Her tongue was a limp lump in her mouth; nerves and feelings were working their way into her face. "Yes," she finally managed. "The Beast will not consume our worlds. Your people are safe. The Rel here is dead … There were other smaller scions in the Slithmet outside."

"We burned them all," Mallel said. He stood and slowly pulled Tara up with him. "And you kept yourself? You did not succumb to the power of the Beast?"

Tara giggled in delirium. "Yes," she said, "I had all of that power at my fingertips, and you know me. I was going to do all of the things. Over tax the poor, enslave an army of destruction, line up all of the attractive men and have my pick of them!" She cackled, looking at Mallel with mocking eyes. "You know me!"

Mallel laughed with her, a deep sound that thundered from his chest. "Hah! That's great," he said, and then, hesitating as quickly as it slipped out, "I love you …"

Tara stopped laughing. Mallel stood rock still; his last laugh caught in his chest and died.

The Luck Symbioid tingled and flared and raged. "I ..." Tara started, but words failed her.

She wrapped her arms around his neck and kissed him, hanging from his shoulders; he wrapped his arms around her waist and held her close, returning the kiss.

Tara was falling again, and she surrendered to the feeling of uncontrolled bliss and ecstasy. She held onto that feeling with Mallel for a beautiful, wondrous forever, until finally her words found her again with a soft fluttering in her heart.

She pulled back reluctantly; she had something to say. "I love you too."

His smile could have silenced the Three Perversities. The hard, stoic leader she knew and respected dissolved into the gorgeous man he was never allowed to embody until just then.

"Ahem." Tara and Mallel started, turning on the breach in the inner skull to find Votly emerging out of the crawlspace. Her arm was held against her chest by a makeshift sling and her skin was pale, but she was alive. "Ah, as thrilled as I am that you two finally got together, and yes, I'm assuming you stopped the Rel first. But our forces have scattered the Slithnet, and now we're being surrounded by immune cells."

"Oh!" Tara dashed away from Mallel and dived into the hole. "I can let them know we mean no harm ... I think."

CHAPTER 21

The *Motebeam*

When Tara commanded the Custanguin to stand down around the hopelessly depleted crew of the *Motebeam*, it wasn't so much a communication as it was an understanding.

She had scrambled out of the crawlspace to find a group of prism marines, riflemen, and an assortment of the odd alien allies backing up against the central skull node. The Custanguin had encircled them.

The battlefield was chaos; the *Motebeam* listed and smouldered, its cannons sizzling and inert as the floors were splattered with shrapnel, viscera, and the corpses of a whole manner of combatants. But now the fighting had died down, and the final two factions were squaring off against one another. As it was, it was not going to be a protracted fight.

"Wait!" Tara sped through her ally's ranks and stood before the towering guardians with her hands splayed out, and they hesitated.

She gazed at them, and they gazed back with their featureless, faceless expressions.

And then, without comment or command, they stood back, making their way back to the shattered wall of the skull to shore up the defences.

Tara turned to face her beleaguered comrades, who stared back at her in wonder. Behind them, Votly and Mallel struggled out of the broken crawlspace, and Mallel donned his thick coat.

Tara's eyes flittered over her allies. Someone was missing.

"Votly," Tara called, resisting the urge to collapse. "Where is Snipes? Did you not pick him up as you rallied the surviving crew?"

Tara knew that not all of the crew members would have been picked up in the *Motebeam's* mad dash to the skull, but she faltered at the way Votly looked back at her and then at the *Motebeam*.

With her breath in her throat, Tara turned and sprinted towards the *Motebeam* with Mallel and Votly hot on her heels.

Tara tore across the battlefield, up the loading rampart, and through the all but empty, ruined chrome hallways of the *Motebeam*. She did not know exactly where to go, but she decided to go for the bridge, and the Luck Symbioid tingled warmly in agreement.

She burst into the marred bridge, and her heart stopped.

There was a figure lying prone next to the helm. A maroon red Hired Heroes' cloak was strewn over the form, concealing their face.

"Oh." Tara stepped over to the body and collapsed on her knees.

"He died upon impact." Tara hadn't noticed there was a group of bridge officers in the room. She hadn't really heard them speak, but they kept going. "The *Motebeam* couldn't course-correct, the damage was so great. He stayed at the helm and directed it through the orbital and magnetic paths mid-flight. He treated the *Motebeam* like it was a bullet and refused to strap in lest we missed the skull ... I'm sorry."

"Tara!" Votly burst into the bridge shortly after Mallel did, who stood stock-still behind her. "Tara, I'm sorry, we were in battle. I didn't have time to ..."

"Shh," Tara said softly.

This was your fault. She wasn't thinking about Votly. She directed the accusation internally, towards herself and the Luck Symbioid. *I gave in to your tingling while Cronetta was strangling me, even though I knew it could affect someone I cared about like this ... I ...* The Luck Symbioid was tingling meekly, not seeking her forgiveness, not seeking to explain to her what it had done.

"It was his choice." Votly's voice finally cut through her ruminations. "I begged him to strap down, but he said this was how he would atone for his sins. He was very brave."

The tingling died down, and Tara took a long, drawn-out, shuddering breath. "It was his choice ..." *He had a choice.*

"Do not blame yourself, Tara." Mallel placed his hand on her shoulder and squeezed. "He knew what he was doing."

It was his choice ... It wasn't the Luck Symbioid manipulating him into it. It wasn't me giving in to luck.

I can't rob him of the decisions he made of his own accord. "He was a hero," Tara finally said. "He saved the world with his sacrifice, many worlds. He told me he came on this voyage to atone for the wrongs he had done in his past."

"I would say he did more than that." Mallel crouched down next to her. "We will honour him."

Tara nodded as the tingling sensation of the Luck Symbioid died down in her awareness, and exhaustion and release washed over her. Tears flowed freely down her face, but she was too tired to sob. She fell into Mallel's arms and let oblivion take her.

* * *

The next few days were a buzz of activity. The Custanguin dragged the *Motebeam* out of the skull as they repaired the cracked bone walls, leaving the Prismath to their own devices upon the spine.

The Slithmet and their war parties had been routed. The ship's scans indicated that all of the Rel Scions had been annihilated in the battle. So the Prismath could freely traverse to the other worlds and communities via the gondolas for supplies and assistance in repairing the ship.

The *Motebeam* had seen better days, but after weeks of work it was space-worthy once more. It was a matter of logistics to traverse the Beast to round up the scattered crew members, including Flayr. She was ferried through great pours in the skin by the tribe Snipes had left her with. They did this as a form of payment after a strange-looking eyeball creature relayed what Snipes had done for them.

There was a service for the fallen, including Snipes, Balt, the other marines, and even the mutineers who had passed in the fighting. The riflemen stood disarmed at the back of the assembly in the cargo hold as the bodies were interred in chrome coffins. They were then stored in the bowels of the ship for a proper sendoff once they made planet fall.

The riflemen and their supporters had atonements to make— that much was clear—but Mallel had spared them from harsh punishment. Their penance was to work the ship as civilians under guard until they could gain the trust of the crew on an individual basis. After Votly showed them the evidence of their folly, they took to their punishment with solemn gratitude.

Tara believed their reactions, but she knew that their trust would never be restored. Their betrayal had weakened the *Motebeam* irreparably, and its mission was still incomplete. The Rel and its Scions were still out there.

Finally, it was time to leave the Beast.

The chrome hull glistened as the amber sails spread and caught the distant sunlight. Thrumming with energy once more, the *Motebeam* lurched and lifted from the base of the skull. The Beast—the Great One—passed beneath the ship as it carried on in its path out of the sun well, with its trailing worlds orbiting in its wake.

Tara watched it leave from the view screen in the bridge. Mallel stood by her side. "What now?" she asked.

She watched Votly take command and give out orders to the rest of the bridge. She waved her injured arm with every order, which was gloved in thick leather and supported by her repaired Light Gauntlet. She was fitting into her new confidence nicely.

Mallel watched on with silent pride, lacing his fingers through Tara's as he sidled up to her. "There is more out there than we realised."

"And less," Tara said as the Beast dwindled into the great expanding void. "When I was connected to the Beast's mind, it was like the galaxy was once a thriving space. Now it's the remnants of a battlefield. The Rel talked about the Symdians again and their Guardians … there is more out there in this conflict than we know, Mallel, and we are woefully unprepared to face what may be coming next."

"And so we shall have to explore, find answers, and investigate," Mallel responded. "We cannot fight our enemy as ill prepared as we are. We have gotten by recently solely from the sacrifices of great people and from your tenacious fighting spirit." He sighed. "But it can't all be up to you, it isn't fair."

"Yes, but I have my rope dart now." Tara patted the weapon coiled on her hip with a smirk. "I will need some training with it, though. Fancy a spar later?"

Mallel's brow furrowed. "You mean a bath?"

Tara giggled. "No, you moon rock moron, a training match."

Mallel chuckled. "Yes, training." He sighed. "We will need much more of it to face the threats to come."

Tara's mirth softened. "What will we do?"

Mallel turned to her, gripping her hand tighter. "Whatever we do, whatever we will face in this wide, uncaring cosmos, we will do it together."

Tara looked at him, "Together," and squeezed his hand back. She turned back to the view screen, laying her head on his shoulder.

Votly smirked at them and then turned away, giving more orders to the bridge crew.

After a moment, Mallel rested his head over Tara's, watching the great starscape beyond.

The Symbicate will return.

A note from the author

Thanks for reading The Symbicate 3!

Your review would make my day! An honest review on Amazon or Goodreads helps other readers find this story, and keeps me writing books for amazing readers like you.

Want more?

Continue the story in *"The Symbicate 4: The Bounty Wars!"* available now!

This is a finished four book series.

Visit SEANMTS.COM to:

- Get a free eBook (and audio stories) when you join the community newsletter

- Read free short stories and articles

- Discover more books you might love

Stay in contact on Instagram: @seanmtshanahan

Email: sean@seanmts.com

If you enjoyed this series, you will love my other books. You can find an up to date list on my site.

Thanks again.

Take care,

Sean

About the Author

Sean M. T. Shanahan is a Science Fiction and Fantasy author from Sydney, Australia. He is known for writing emotionally gripping, high-stakes stories that blend dynamic characters with intriguing concepts and take you through darkness into the light.

He has a lifelong passion for storytelling, and since publishing his first book in 2021 has produced multiple books that span Fantasy, Steampunk, Sci-Fi, and children's fiction.

Drawing inspiration from history, science, mythology, and adventure, he weaves immersive tales that will pull you in from the start and leave you wanting more.

Besides reading and writing, Sean enjoys nature, gaming, parkour, endurance sports, and making terrible jokes.

www.ingramcontent.com/pod-product-compliance
Lightning Source LLC
Chambersburg PA
CBHW040221170726
48295CB00014B/763